D1290181

Two-Boy Cruise

by Bonnie Towne

Published by Willowisp Press®, Inc.
401 E. Wilson Bridge Road, Worthington, Ohio 43085

Copyright ©1986 by Willowisp Press, Inc.

Printed in the United States of America
10 9 8 7 6 5 4 3 2

ISBN 0-87406-149-0

To Alyn
My soul mate

One

"OH, no, that's terrible," my grandmother said, blinking her blue eyes and looking shocked. "Then who's going on the cruise with me?"

"I'm really sorry about the timing," my mom said. "I can't go because my new job starts next week. They need me at the bank sooner than I thought. It just can't be helped, that's all."

"Joan, you know how I've been looking forward to this cruise," my grandmother said to my mother.

"I know you have, Mother, but..."

"Then I repeat, who's going on the cruise with me?" My grandmother slumped into the chair across from me.

I was lying on the couch, listening to this conversation between my grandmother and my mom. Right now, I'd guess the winner to be

Grandmother. She was more upset.

"Let's see, Jimmy is away at camp, so he's out." Mom was thinking aloud, pacing back and forth like she always does. Jimmy's my brother. He's fourteen.

"I've paid two fares, and the cruise is next week," Grandmother reminded Mom. "It's too late to get my money back." She folded her arms.

"I know!" Mom looked inspired. "Niki can go."

"Me?" I liked being a spectator at these discussions. I knew being a participant meant trouble.

My grandmother turned and stared at me.

"Of course, Mother, Niki is the perfect age—thirteen," Mom went on. "You and she are great companions. Think of all the Saturday outings you two have enjoyed. Isn't that right, Niki?"

"Uh, right," I mumbled. How did I get into this conversation anyway? I wondered. And how was I going to get out of it now?

"Well, we do have a good time together." Grandmother hesitated.

"And you'll have a great time on the cruise," Mom insisted. "There's still time to take Niki shopping for her cruise wardrobe."

Mom smiled, and I knew I'd had it. My

grandmother loved to shop more than anything.

"Then it's all settled," Grandmother said, smiling. "Niki has been chosen to accompany me on the *Sun Goddess* cruise to Nassau, San Juan, and St. Thomas." She looked at me like I'd just won a prize.

"Tell your grandmother how excited you are," Mom said, nodding at me.

"Wow, it'll be great." I tried to sound enthusiastic. Did I miss something or was I not consulted in this matter? I wondered.

"I must go. I have some arrangements to make." Grandmother kissed Mom and me and breezed out the door. "I'll call you, Niki, about the shopping trip." The door closed behind her.

"Mom!" I said, indignantly.

She held up her hands. "Niki, I know what you're going to say. I'm sorry I volunteered you without your consent." She paced back and forth. "But you know how much this cruise means to your grandmother. Your grandfather has been dead for seven years now. Your grandmother feels she needs to do something new and have a little fun for a change."

"But, Mom, you could have at least pretended to ask me what I thought," I cried.

"Be happy you've been chosen to go," Mom said, putting her hand gently on my shoulder. "It will be a great experience for you. And thank you for coming to my rescue before my new job starts," she added, hugging me.

The doorbell rang. "I have some calls to make," Mom said. "Get that, will you?" She walked toward her room.

I answered the door. It was Jenny, my best friend since kindergarten. She lives next door. "Am I ever glad to see you," I said.

"What's the matter?" Jenny asked.

"You'll never guess what Isabel and Joan just did to me," I complained, heading for the refrigerator.

Jenny rolled her eyes. "What did they do this time?" I guess she's used to me complaining about my grandmother and my mother.

"They decided without asking me that I'm going on a cruise with my grandmother. Did you ever hear of anything so nerdy in your life?"

"A cruise? Like on *Love Boat*?" Jenny asked, getting a dreamy look in her green eyes. "It sounds romantic to me."

"But with my grandmother? She'll probably interview all the boys on board and try to find me a boyfriend." I got out the big bottle of cola. "Want some?" I asked.

"Yeah, thanks," Jenny said. "At least there will be boys on the cruise, which is more than I can say for around here."

"That's true," I agreed. We observed a moment of silence for the terrible tragedy of our neighborhood. Not one cute boy lived here.

"Think about it, Niki," Jenny said. "You might find a boyfriend, like the girls do on *Love Boat*." Jenny was actually getting excited about MY cruise.

"I think I could handle having a boyfriend," I admitted, smiling.

"And you get to dress up for those fabulous dinners, and dance every night and—"

"Whoa, there." I held up my hands. Jenny was beginning to sound like my mom. "Let's not get carried away. I'm not too excited about the dressing-up part." When you live in Florida, you wear shorts as often as possible. The temperature is always ninety degrees.

"But, Niki, think of what an adventure it will be," Jenny exclaimed. "You'll be doing new things and meeting new people. I wish I were going."

"But with my grandmother? The people will probably be ancient," I groaned.

"Give it a chance, Niki," Jenny urged. "Why

don't you watch the reruns of *Love Boat*? Then you'll see what fun you're going to have."

"Okay, I'll watch them," I said, putting my empty glass in the sink. "But I can't guarantee I'll get excited."

"Let's go pick out what clothes you should take," Jenny suggested. Her green eyes were sparkling now, and her freckles were standing out on her nose.

Even though we're best friends, Jenny and I are opposites in looks. Jenny is blond and fragile-looking. I have brown hair and brown eyes like my dad.

The worst thing about me is that I'm tall. And I have a tendency to get fat if I don't watch it. Boys always seem to go for short girls, not tall ones. I guess that's why I've never had a boyfriend.

"Isabel is taking me on a shopping trip before we leave," I confessed.

"Oh-hhh," Jenny moaned. "Niki, you're so lucky. I can't believe you're complaining. If you say another word about not wanting to go on this cruise, I'll scream."

I laughed sheepishly. "Okay, okay, since I can't talk about the cruise, do you want to play tennis?"

"You're on," Jenny said. "I'll go get my racket."

* * * * *

I guess my heart wasn't really into playing tennis that day. Jenny beat me badly. Then she spent the rest of the week convincing me I was going to love the cruise. When I was with her, I thought I was convinced. But when I was alone, I wasn't so sure.

I remembered plenty of disastrous middle school dances. And I couldn't see myself discussing politics with people my grandmother's age either. There were a lot of drawbacks to this cruise that Jenny refused to consider.

On Wednesday before we left on Friday, Grandmother and I went on a big "chicken salad shopping trip." I call it that because she always takes me to lunch at Harvey's. And she always orders chicken salad.

"Let's see," Isabel said as she stirred cream into her after-lunch coffee. "What have we bought so far?"

"The pink dress and two shorts outfits," I answered. I was about to dig into a hot fudge sundae with nuts, whipped cream, and a cherry.

"Oh, yes, I remember now. We have to buy you a new bathing suit."

"That ought to do it," I said between bites.

My grandmother looked at me. "When I was your age and someone offered to buy me clothes, I let them."

"I guess that's the difference between you and me," I said, smiling.

"I also would have been considered rude if I talked that way to my grandmother," she observed. Her blue eyes sparkled.

"Times have changed," I offered.

"I think we're going to have a wonderful time," Isabel said, chuckling. "If you get bored, I know you'll speak up."

I smiled and shrugged.

"By the way, I think it would be appropriate if you'd call me 'Isabel' on the cruise." She stared at me. "Since you're such a modern granddaughter that shouldn't be too hard, right?"

"No problem," I said. "I'll be happy to call you 'Isabel.'" I didn't tell her that I'd been calling her "Isabel" in my mind for several years now.

* * * * *

After lunch Isabel dragged me into seven stores to find the perfect bathing suit. I kept telling her none of the suits would make me look skinny. She kept telling me to quit eating hot fudge sundaes.

Finally we found a royal blue suit that made my skin look warm and almond-colored. Isabel approved and bought it immediately. Then she announced we were going home.

After she left, I spread my new clothes on my bed. I now owned a pink organza dress that rustled when I walked and made me itch under my arms. I also got some pretty cool shorts and tops. Best of all, I liked the new royal blue swim suit, which made me look almost skinny.

*   *   *   *   *

Friday arrived too quickly. In no time at all, we drove from our home in Fort Lauderdale to the port in Miami. Dad and Mom talked about what a good time Isabel and I were going to have. Jenny came along. She kept babbling about all the boys I was going to meet.

"There she is, Niki," Isabel exclaimed, "the *Sun Goddess.* Isn't she beautiful?"

"Wow," I whispered.

The ship was completely white, like a graceful swan sitting on the water. The portholes were like tiny dots on her side.

"It's bigger than it looked in the pictures," Jenny said.

"It's wonderful," Isabel said. "Oh, Niki, we're going to have such a good time."

"I'll let you out here, and I'll park the car," Dad offered.

"Good idea," Mom said.

As we scrambled out and grabbed our bags, I kept staring at the *Sun Goddess*. It was more glamorous than I had ever imagined. It made me nervous to think about living on such a beautiful ship for a week.

We struggled up the gangplank with our bags. Two members of the cruise staff met us and gave us directions to our cabin. They seemed like regular people, not at all like the crew on *Love Boat*.

While we were waiting for Dad, we peeked into the lounges. The highly polished wood paneling and green velvet chairs looked so luxurious. Dad arrived and gave my hand a squeeze. I must have looked nervous.

"We have to go down two floors," Mom said, heading for the stairs. Our cabin was on the Riviera Deck.

"Let's see." Isabel took the lead. "It should be down this hall somewhere."

I paused, trying to read the numbers on the doors.

"Excuse me, do you know where cabin 162 is?" someone behind me asked.

I turned around. A boy with lots of reddish-blond hair was staring at me.

"No, I'm looking for my cabin, too," I said.

"Maybe the even numbers are on the other side of the hall," he said, walking across to another door.

I wasn't sure what to do. I didn't see Isabel or my parents anywhere. I watched the boy, fascinated. He had bright blue eyes and a huge zit on the end of his nose. His hair was curly and fine and stuck out in all directions like a halo.

"Niki, I found it." Isabel stuck her head out from a cabin down the hall.

"Well, good luck," I said to the boy. "I guess we've found our cabin." I pointed at Isabel.

"Oh . . . , my name is Craig Nelson." He gave me a little wave as if he didn't know what to do with his hands. "I'll see you around . . . if I ever find my cabin, that is." He laughed nervously.

"Good luck," I said again and started down the hall. This guy seemed a little strange, but at least he was as tall as I was. That was a plus.

"See you later," Craig called as I entered our cabin.

"So long," I said without looking at him.

The cabin was small, but as luxurious as the

rest of the ship. The walls were light gray, and the carpet was a slightly darker shade of gray. The two twin beds and two chairs were covered in peach velvet.

"Who was that?" Jenny wanted to know. She sat in one of the chairs next to a small table with a fruit basket on it.

"Some nerdy boy with a zit on his nose," I answered.

"Niki!" Dad said. He looked at Mom and they both laughed. The adults were munching on a plate of hors d'oeuvres that had been left to welcome us to the ship.

"Well, at least I saw one cute boy," Jenny said, smiling.

"Where?" I asked, quicker than I meant to.

"On the stairs. He was tall and had dark hair and a beautiful tan."

"What's his name and his cabin number?" I asked.

"Sorry you'll have to do that detective work yourself," Jenny teased.

"If he's that good looking, I'll find him," I boasted.

"Remember, you're going to sit at this table and write me a letter every day," Jenny said.

"I'll remember," I said, smiling.

The whistle blew and a message came over the loudspeaker that all visitors had to leave the ship. My family and Jenny hugged Isabel and me good-bye. Then Isabel and I looked at each other. Without Jenny here to tease me into being bold, I didn't feel quite as confident.

Two

"WE'D better unpack tonight," Isabel suggested after we'd said good-bye to my parents. "The ship docks in Nassau in the morning."

"Okay," I said, opening the closet door. "The closets sure are tiny."

"They are, indeed!" Isabel agreed. "Look at these drawers. There's certainly no wasted space in this cabin."

We had just started putting our things away when the loudspeaker came on. "All passengers will report to their designated deck wearing their lifejackets," the voice said.

"Oh, fiddlesticks," Isabel fumed. "Not a lifeboat drill now. I'm in the middle of unpacking."

"I think it's required," I reminded her. Anyway, a lifeboat drill might be a good way to meet the cute guy Jenny had told me about, I thought.

"All right, let's go," Isabel sighed. "I hope it won't take long."

We found out lifejackets in an overhead compartment. Stenciled on the compartment door was the name of the deck where we were supposed to go. We climbed the stairs and went out on deck with the other passengers.

I searched the crowd for Jenny's cute guy. Suddenly someone walked past and caught my eye. It was him! I was sure of it.

My heart started to pound. He was tall with wavy brown hair and a gorgeous tan. He had on a pink surfing shirt and white slacks, and he looked terrific.

"Niki, is it my imagination or are you staring at that young man over there?" Isabel asked in an amused tone.

"What?" I turned around. "Oh, no, I'm not staring. I'm just checking him out." I smiled, guiltily.

Isabel chuckled. "I'll remember that, 'just checking him out.' "

I stared at him some more. I kept visualizing the two of us at the beach having a great time together. It's amazing what your imagination can do when you have the right raw material to work with.

When the lifeboat drill was over, I reluctantly followed Isabel back to our cabin.

But who wanted to unpack when there was a cute boy to think about? I had to find a way to meet him.

"I think we should get a good night's sleep, don't you, Niki?" Isabel asked.

"I guess so," I said.

"We want to be ready for the Straw Market in Nassau early in the morning," Isabel said.

To Isabel shopping was an athletic event. I didn't need to save my energy for shopping, that was for sure. Now I had to wait until tomorrow to meet my wavy-haired guy.

I quickly finished unpacking. Then I got into bed and stared at the ceiling. I hoped this cruise wasn't going to turn out to be a week-long, glorified shopping trip.

* * * * *

The next morning at breakfast, Isabel and I were seated at a table close to the window. The sun shone, and the clear, emerald green ocean seemed to rise and fall on the horizon. It was beautiful.

"The sea air always makes me hungry," Isabel said, glancing at her menu.

"We live near the ocean," I said, giggling. "That must mean you're always hungry."

Isabel lowered her menu to give me a dead

pan stare. "Don't confuse me with logic, Niki."

I laughed and looked at my menu. I ordered French toast.

All during breakfast Isabel talked about going into Nassau. I thought about my cute guy. I just had to meet him. But how to meet him was the big question.

When we'd finished eating, Isabel went on deck to watch our approach to Nassau. I decided to check out the Teen Room.

I had to ask directions three times and walk through two lounges to find it. I was beginning to appreciate how big this ship really was.

It was worth the walk, however, to see the Teen Room. It was decorated in purple and pink and had a real dance floor in the center. Hearing rock music made me feel relaxed and at home.

Then I saw him. Jenny's cute guy was sitting at a table with some other kids and a gorgeous blond girl. When I saw her, I knew he was already taken.

The girl's hair was long and perfectly curled around her face. She wore blue eye shadow and lots of eyeliner, which made her look super sophisticated. She must be at least sixteen, I thought.

My wavy-haired guy was smiling at her and listening to her talk. I guess I must have been staring at them.

"Hi, I'm Hilary," the blond girl said, turning to me. "Want to sit with us?"

"Sure," I said. "My name is Niki." I slipped into a purple plastic chair next to Hilary.

"This is Candy and Travis," Hilary said, introducing me to a pretty dark-haired girl with dimples and a big guy who looked like a football player. They both said, "hi."

"Hi," I said.

"I'm Darren." My cute boy smiled at me.

"I think I saw you at the lifeboat drill," I said, smiling my biggest smile.

"Yeah, you look familiar," he said.

"How about that lifeboat drill?" Hilary asked. "Nobody knew what was going on."

"Yeah," Candy agreed. "We could have tried on our lifejackets in our cabins."

"Where are you from?" Darren asked me.

"Fort Lauderdale," I answered. He kept looking at me. Of course, I was kind of staring at him, too.

"Did you two know each other?" I asked Hilary and Darren.

"No," Hilary said. "We just met. I'm from Tampa, and Darren's from Daytona Beach."

A new song started on the juke box. Hilary said she didn't like it, which started a discussion about our favorite rock groups. We all liked different rock stars except for Travis, who liked country music. He was from Alabama.

All the time, Darren kept looking at me. My heart was pounding so loud that I was beginning to get embarrassed.

"You sure have a good tan," I said to Darren.

"Yeah, I surf a lot," he said.

I loved the way he smiled. Looking at him gave me goose bumps. "A lot of kids surf at Lauderdale," I said.

"Guys from all over the state drive to Daytona Beach to surf," Darren said.

"That's true," Candy added, smiling.

Hilary rolled her eyes and looked at Travis. She didn't seem to be as fascinated with Darren as I was. She put her chin on her hand and her chunky bracelets jangled.

Then the loudspeaker blared that the ship had docked at Nassau and the passengers could go ashore.

"Niki, are you going into Nassau?" Hilary asked.

"Sure," I said. "That's the thing to do, I guess."

"Well, we'll have to get together," Darren said, rising and flashing his dazzling smile at me as he left. "I'll see you later on the Promenade Deck."

24

"I'd better go," Candy said, getting up to leave.

"I have to go, too," Travis said. "My mom wants me to carry all those baskets she's going to buy."

"Sounds like Darren was pretty impressed with you," Hilary said after the rest had left.

"Oh, I don't know," I said, even though I was secretly pleased with her words.

I told Hilary good-bye and practically ran back to my cabin to get ready. Darren didn't say what time he'd meet me. I wanted to look gorgeous and yet not keep him waiting. That meant I had to hurry.

"Niki, there you are, dear." Isabel looked distracted like she always does when she's going shopping. "Hurry and get ready. We can go ashore now, you know."

"I know," I said. "But I met a boy named Darren. He asked me to go ashore with him. It's all right, isn't it?"

"Well, I guess so," Isabel said, slowly. "I met this delightful woman, Gloria. She asked me to go to Nassau with her. I know you'd get bored with all the shopping. Sure, go ahead and join the young people."

Isabel hugged me and left. I went through my clothes a million times, trying to decide what to wear.

"Why didn't I let Isabel buy me more clothes?" I groaned. I finally settled on my white skirt and blue and white top. They made me look skinny and, I hoped, older. I tried not to think about how sophisticated Hilary looked compared to me.

When I got to the Promenade Deck, Isabel and Gloria were getting ready to depart.

"Are you sure you don't want to come with us?" Isabel asked after she'd introduced me to Gloria. Like Isabel, Gloria was short and white-haired and seemed anxious to go shopping.

"No, Darren will be along any minute," I said. I looked around for him. He left the Teen Room before I did, so he should be here by now, I thought.

"Perhaps we should wait and meet the young man," Isabel said.

"You go ahead," I insisted. "I'll be all right." I sure didn't want Isabel to interrogate Darren.

"Well, if you're sure. . . ." Isabel looked at her watch and gave me a hug. I could tell she really wanted to leave.

"I'm sure. Have a good time." I waved good-bye, trying to be cheerful. Actually, I felt very nervous about meeting Darren.

I watched Isabel and Gloria walk down the gangplank and grow smaller and smaller. I kept telling myself that Darren would be here any minute. But as more and more people passed me by, I knew I was wrong.

I sat down on a lounge chair. Maybe I had been mistaken about Darren's invitation. I went over our conversation so many times, I forgot who had said what. When I realized I was the only passenger left on the ship, I couldn't stop the tears from flowing.

I spent the rest of the day sunning myself on the Lido Deck and paddling around in the pool. Swimming wasn't very much fun by myself. All in all, I had a pretty miserable day.

Later I wrote to Jenny. I couldn't bring myself to tell her what really happened.

Dear Jenny,

I'm having a wonderful time. You'll never guess who I met in the Teen Room. Darren, the cute guy you saw. He's really neat. He's a surfer from Daytona Beach.

Darren's taking me to the Straw Market in Nassau today. I'll tell you all about it when I get home. Thank goodness there are more boys on this cruise then there are in our neighborhood.

So long for now,

Niki

While I was dressing for dinner, Isabel burst in, her arms loaded with straw baskets.

"Look what bargains I found," she said, awkwardly setting down her purchases.

"I'm sure the Straw Market had a good day," I said.

"What's the matter, dear? You sound depressed." Isabel felt my forehead for fever.

"I'm okay," I said. "It's just that Darren never showed up. I spent the whole day aboard the ship all alone."

"Oh, dear." Isabel sank into one of the peach chairs. "I was afraid something like that would happen. I shouldn't have been in such a hurry to leave you."

"It's not your fault," I said. "I should have made sure it was a real invitation."

"I feel so bad," Isabel went on.

"I had a good day, really," I said. "I worked on my tan." I hoped I sounded convincing. I didn't want Isabel to blame herself for my stupidity.

Isabel smiled and gave me a hug. "We'll have to find you another young man . . . one who appreciates you."

Oh, no, I thought. That's all I need is to have Isabel recruiting boyfriends for me!

* * * * *

Dinner was another exercise in patience. We sat through four courses. It was delicious, though. Or maybe it tasted good because I was extra hungry. They had all my favorites— French onion soup, salad, filet mignon, and Black Forest cake.

I was right about the people at our table. Everyone had white hair but me. They talked about politics and the Straw Market. And I didn't have anything to say about either.

After dessert I saw Hilary across the room. She waved at me and motioned for me to join her. I nodded.

"Niki, you'll have to excuse me," Isabel said, when we'd finished. "I'm so exhausted, I'm going to turn in. I promise I'll be better company tomorrow night."

"It's okay," I said. "I think I'll go for a walk with my new friend." I introduced Hilary to my grandmother.

Isabel looked relieved. "I'm happy to meet you, Hilary." She turned to me. "Of course, Niki. Go along and have a good time."

"Okay," I said. "I won't be too late."

Hilary and I walked out to the deck and looked up at the millions of stars.

"Never go on a cruise with your grandmother," I said.

"What interesting advice," Hilary said. "I'll

remember it the next time my grandmother suggests a cruise."

I giggled. "What I mean is, grandmothers only want to shop all day and go to bed at nine-thirty."

"So? Now you can do what you want," Hilary said. "My parents are in one of the lounges, and I have to check in with them every so often. That's worse."

"Maybe you're right," I said. "I hadn't thought of that."

"Why don't we go to the Teen Room?" Hilary asked. "My hair is getting limp in this damp air."

"I'm afraid I'll see Darren," I blurted out. I took a deep breath. Then I told Hilary what had happened with Darren today.

"Those things happen," Hilary said. "But I wouldn't let a little misunderstanding keep me from dancing." She looked up at the stars.

"Maybe I shouldn't." I wished powerfully that Jenny were here right now. I wanted to tell my problems to my best friend that I'd known since kindergarten. She would be much more sympathetic than a stranger named Hilary. Suddenly I felt very homesick and overwhelmed by this big cruise ship.

"I guess I'll go find my parents and then go to the Teen Room," Hilary said. "Sure you don't want to come along?"

"No, I'm a little tired anyway. I guess I'll just turn in early," I said. "See you tomorrow."

I went down the steps to my cabin, tears slipping down my cheeks with each step. I was mad at Darren for not showing up, and I was mad at myself for misunderstanding his invitation. I was even mad at Jenny for talking me into coming on this rotten cruise. I had six more days of this horrible trip to get through. How could she have done this to me?

Three

AT breakfast the next morning I was already depressed, and then the worst thing happened. I saw Craig, that nerdy kid. He stood across the dining room waving his arms at me. I turned around to see what was going on behind me, but there was no one there. So I gave him the tiniest wave back. What was I supposed to do, ignore him?

"Oh, no," I said out loud.

"What is it, dear?" Isabel asked.

"It's Craig Nelson," I said. "He's coming over here!" I wanted to disappear.

"He looks like a nice sort," Isabel said, encouragingly.

"Uh, Isabel, this is Craig Nelson," I said. "Craig, my grandmother, Mrs. Sloane."

"How do you do, Mrs. Sloane?" Craig said to Isabel. "Are you enjoying your cruise?"

"It's delightful," Isabel said. "Won't you sit

down with us for a while?"

Craig pulled up a chair and continued talking with Isabel. I tried to figure what it was that I didn't like about him. I guess it was that he tried too hard to be friendly. Nobody I knew tried that hard. They were too busy being cool.

"Niki," Craig said, turning to me. "There's a tour of the bridge this morning. It starts in just a few minutes. Would you like to go?"

"This morning? Well, I. . . ." I didn't know what to say.

"Of course, you go right along, Niki," Isabel said, in her most soothing voice. "I'm planning to go to the arts and crafts lecture this morning anyway. I'll meet you back here for lunch."

"Well, all right." What else could I say?

Isabel stood up, and Craig actually sprang up to pull back her chair. I groaned inwardly. Was this going to be another wasted day? What a nightmare this cruise was turning out to be.

"You young people have a marvelous morning," Isabel said, gaily. I could tell she thought she had fixed me up with a "nice young man."

"You, too," I said. She kissed my cheek and shook hands with Craig.

Craig and I went upstairs to the Lido Deck where the tour started. "Your grandmother is very nice," he observed.

"That's what all the boys say," I said.

Craig laughed. "What's your favorite color?"

"My favorite color? Blue. Why?" I asked. I had a horrible sinking feeling. What if we ran into Darren on this tour? I couldn't imagine anything worse. I tried to stand at the back of the crowd that had gathered for the tour, hoping I wouldn't be noticed.

Craig kept right on talking. "Mine's green. I have a theory about people that like each other. They really have lots in common in spite of the old saying that opposites attract."

"Really? Sounds interesting." I searched the crowd for Darren's face.

"The real reason people don't think they have anything in common is that they don't do enough research," Craig observed.

"Research?" I didn't understand.

"Either that or they really don't know themselves." Craig chuckled.

A handsome man in ship's uniform emerged from the doorway and began to talk about the ship. Craig listened some and then went right on talking. Between the man and Craig, I was getting a real education.

"What's your favorite flavor of ice cream?"

Craig whispered as we entered the bridge.

"I like hot fudge sundaes," I whispered back, staring at the huge wheel. A burly man stood behind it. Even though he had both hands on the wheel, it never seemed to move.

"Aha," Craig said too loudly. Everyone on the tour turned to glare at him.

"Sorry," he waved good-naturedly at the people. Out of the side of his mouth he whispered to me, "Hot fudge sundaes are my favorite, too."

I giggled in spite of myself. He seemed so proud of his finding.

"Where are you from?" he asked.

"Fort Lauderdale," I said. "How about you?"

"Miami," he said. "That's almost a match."

Our tour guide was spouting all kinds of numbers—how fast the ship goes, how much water it displaces, that it weighs 45,000 tons. Numbers always impressed me.

"What are your favorite courses in school?" Craig asked, not listening to the figures.

"History," I said. "But I kind of like computer science, too."

"Aha." Craig whispered it this time. "I took computer science last year, and I loved it. I want to be a computer engineer."

I smiled. Completely forgetting about the

tour, I said, "I bet your father's not an insurance broker."

"No, he's in the wholesale jewelry business." Craig thought for a minute. "But my mother's a loan officer in a bank."

"My mother works in a bank, too," I exclaimed. "She's in the public relations department."

People glared at me this time. Craig suppressed a giggle. "What's your favorite spectator sport?" he asked.

"Tennis," I answered. We were outside the working deck now. The officer was talking about rope.

"Wow," Craig said. "What's your favorite participant sport?"

"Tennis," I said. "My whole family loves tennis."

"Wow," Craig exclaimed. "I love tennis. I come from a family of tennis nuts, too."

On that one we giggled so much that we had to leave the tour. We ran down two flights of stairs until we were far enough away from the tour to giggle our hearts out.

"Tennis has never been this funny before," Craig confessed.

"Never," I agreed, still giggling.

"I guess we weren't paying much attention to the tour anyway," Craig said, still laughing.

"Want to take a walk around this deck?"

"Okay." I pushed my hair out of my face.

Suddenly I got self-conscious about being with Craig. I worried about seeing Darren.

"Why don't we find a lounge chair and sit down for a while?" I suggested. I sneaked a look at my watch. It would be time to meet Isabel in half an hour.

"Suits me," Craig said, smiling. He pulled up two lounge chairs and sat down on one. I sat on the other.

"So what do you think of my theory now?" Craig tried to regain our giggling mood, but the magic was gone.

"I think your theory is right on," I said, trying to sound enthusiastic.

We sat for a while not talking. The sun felt warm on my body. The waves splashing against the side of the ship lulled me into feeling drowsy. It felt like Craig and I were floating all alone on the big ship.

The chime which announced the first lunch sitting broke into my thoughts. Not everyone on the ship could fit in the dining room at the same time. So there were two sittings an hour and a half apart for each meal.

"I'm supposed to meet Isabel now," I said, jumping up.

"Yeah, I have to meet my parents, too,"

Craig said. "I'll see you later, Niki. I had a good time this morning."

"Me, too," I said.

Craig waved his silly little wave and took off. I walked to the dining room, thinking about Craig and smiling.

"Here we are, Niki, over here," Isabel called. "You must have had a nice morning to be smiling like that."

"Yes, I did." My smile faded. There was Isabel with an older man, another couple, and Darren. What was Darren doing at our table?

"Niki, I'd like you to meet Tom Stewart." Isabel steered me to the older gentleman. "And this is George Wright and his wife, Doris, and their son, Darren. Everyone, this is my granddaughter, Niki."

Everyone said hello, but all I saw was Darren. He was smiling at me. "Niki and I have already met," Darren said.

"Wonderful," Isabel said. "Niki, you've been keeping things from me."

Everyone laughed and picked up their menus. I was still staring at Darren. What was I going to do now?

Darren acted like nothing had happened. I was still plenty mad at him for standing me up. But maybe he hadn't really invited me to go to Nassau with him. I was still very confused about yesterday.

"Your grandmother tells me you're going to be in the ninth grade," Tom said.

"Yes," I answered.

"Do you start a language in ninth grade at your school?" Tom asked.

"I've already had two years of Spanish," I said. Suddenly, I wondered if Craig had studied Spanish, too.

"Niki does very well in school," Isabel said, winking at me.

"I'm sure she does," Tom said as the waiter began to take our orders.

"Darren is going to be in tenth grade," his mother said. "He's taking all the science he can get."

"I thought Darren wanted to major in surfing," his father said.

"Now, dear," Doris said.

"Mom, you told him." Darren acted betrayed. I got a thrill when he smiled.

Tom and George started talking about fishing. Darren grinned at me, and I must confess I grinned back.

During lunch I concluded he hadn't meant to invite me yesterday. And I was too embarrassed to mention it.

"Why don't you young people go for a walk after lunch?" Isabel suggested as she took the last sip of her coffee.

"Good idea," Darren said, smiling at me. "Want to go for a walk, young person?"

I giggled. "Okay." What else could I say?

"We're going to play bridge this afternoon," Doris said to Darren. "If you need us, we'll be in the Carnival Lounge."

"Okay, Mom. I'll see you later," Darren said.

He held out his hand to me, and I preceded him out onto the deck. My heart was beating so fast. I searched my brain for something clever to say. It makes me so mad when I get shy around cute boys.

"Where do you want to walk?" Darren asked.

"It doesn't matter," I answered quickly. "Here is fine." Great, Niki, what a stupid answer, I thought.

"Want to walk around the pool and see what's happening?" Darren asked.

"Sure." We walked out to the pool and circled it. The sun was warm on my head, and the wind messed up my hair. Darren's wavy hair stood up a little in the breeze, but he still looked great.

"This is sure good surfing weather," Darren said, watching the waves. "See those white caps? They'd be full-blown waves on the beach."

"Oh." I stared at the waves. "My brother Jimmy surfs."

"Really? What kind of board does he have?"

"I don't know," I said. I felt awkward talking to Darren. I couldn't think of anything to say. I was beginning to think I was antisocial. What did other girls talk to Darren about?

"Do you play sports in school?" I asked.

"Yeah, cross country and track," Darren said, smiling. "My dad keeps talking about a running scholarship."

"That sounds good." I leaned against the railing.

"I really don't want it," Darren said. "I don't want to run in college. There are too many other things to do."

"I know what you mean," I said. I could smell his cologne. He was so close to me, I thought I would faint.

"Want to walk around the deck the other way?" Darren asked.

"Sure," I said. We walked into the wind, feeling it snatch our breath away. We didn't talk.

When we got to the other side, the wind lessened. There was a swimsuit fashion show near the tables. We stopped to watch for a while.

I knew there must be something wrong with

me. What other reason could there be for not being able to talk to the cutest guy I'd ever met?

I looked up and felt sick. Craig was coming straight toward us.

"Let's walk this way," I suggested to Darren. But it was too late. Craig had seen us.

"Hey, Niki, how's it going?" Craig asked with a big smile. "Hi, Craig Nelson's the name." He shook hands with Darren.

Darren introduced himself. All I could do was stare at Craig in horror.

"Say, Niki, we forgot to check out our favorite rock groups," Craig went on. "We'll do that the next time, maybe tonight in the Teen Room. Save me a couple of dances, will you?" Craig sauntered off before I could say a word.

"Is he a friend of yours?" Darren asked.

"No." I managed to find my voice. "I just met him. His cabin is down the hall from mine."

"I think I've had enough walking for today. Let's sit down for a while," Darren suggested, collapsing on the closest lounge chair.

"Okay." I sat down beside him. I was so furious with Craig I couldn't talk. I rehearsed in my mind how to tell him to leave me alone.

"Do you have plans for this afternoon?" Darren asked.

"No," I said. Then I remembered Craig was going to play tennis. I didn't want to show up on the tennis court with Darren and run into Craig again.

"Maybe I'll go swimming," I said in my most cheerful voice. "Doesn't that sound like a good idea?"

Darren's smile faded. "Sounds good, all right. But I made plans to play tennis. Looks like I'll have to take a rain check on the swim." He smiled at me and left.

I closed my eyes and made a horrible face. I felt like screaming, What a fool you are, Niki! I knew what I'd done the minute I mentioned swimming. I should have let him say what he was doing first.

I seemed to have a talent for doing the wrong thing where Darren was concerned. This time I blamed it all on Craig for making me so flustered.

I lay there feeling sorry for myself until the sun got too hot. Then I plodded down to my cabin. It was cool and dark. I sat down and wrote a letter to Jenny:

Dear Jenny,

   You'll never believe what happened today. First I got stuck into taking a tour of the bridge with Craig. He played this dumb game which made us so hysterical that we almost got thrown out of the tour. I laughed so much my sides ached.

Then guess who Isabel was having lunch with? Darren and his parents. Darren and I went for a walk afterward. He is so-o-o good-looking, and his cologne is so-o-o divine.

Then that nerd Craig came up to us and acted like he was my best buddy. I couldn't believe it. I was so embarrassed.

But the worst part was when Darren asked me what I was doing this afternoon. I said swimming, but he had already planned to play tennis. When will I ever learn to keep my mouth shut?

I wish you were here to advise me in this mess.

So long for now,

Niki

Four

AFTER I put my letter to Jenny in the dresser, I decided to go swimming. "I certainly don't need Darren to have fun on this cruise," I told myself.

On the Lido Deck I saw Hilary lounging near the pool reading a book. She noticed me and waved. "Hey, Niki, come on over. Here's an empty chair."

I grabbed the chaise and sat down. "Thanks," I said. "A person could wait all day for a place to sit."

"Don't mention it," Hilary said. "Do you think I'm getting any sun?"

"I think you're getting a lot. Your tan looks great with that white bikini," I said. "Want some of my oil?" I generously spread oil all over my body.

"No, thanks, I did that in the cabin," Hilary said.

Whenever she said anything she gestured with her hands. I noticed her slender fingers and her flawless red nail polish.

"So do you think we'll have any fun on this cruise?" Hilary asked. "I must confess I came on this trip expecting to be bored out of my mind." She gestured again.

"I don't know," I said. "I've had some boring moments myself. But I keep hoping something exciting will happen."

"I think you're an optimist, Niki," Hilary said, laughing.

"How old are you?" I asked.

"Fourteen."

"Going into the ninth grade?"

"Yes, why?"

"I just wondered. You look older," I admitted.

"Everybody tells me that." Hilary gave another throaty laugh. "Are you going into ninth grade, too?"

"Yes. I'm a little worried about high school," I said. "The one I'm going to is so big."

"I go to private school," Hilary said. "It's small and I've been going there for eight years already."

"Oh, so you're a private school snob!" I blurted out before I thought.

Hilary's face changed immediately. She took

off her sunglasses and looked at me earnestly. "Do you really think so? I try hard not to be one."

"Oh, no, I'm sorry," I quickly explained. "I didn't really mean YOU were a snob. It's just that most public school kids think private school kids are snobs."

Hilary settled back in her chair and replaced her glasses. "Some of the girls at my school really are snobs."

I was getting a different picture of Hilary now. I had wondered if she were really human. I mean the girl doesn't even sweat. But if she cared whether I thought she was a snob, maybe she was okay after all.

I turned over on my stomach and propped up my chin with my hand. "Have you met any cute guys on this cruise?"

"No, this ship is mostly the pits as far as boys are concerned, except for Darren, that is. And he already has eyes for you."

I giggled. "I don't know about Darren," I confided.

"What's not to know?" Hilary peered at me over the tops of her glasses.

"I can't find a thing to talk to him about," I complained.

"Who needs to talk?" Hilary laughed. "Just looking at those gorgeous, tanned muscles should keep you busy."

"You know what I mean," I said, giggling. "He might lose interest if all I do is stare at him."

"So dance with him. You don't have to talk while you're dancing, do you?" Hilary asked.

"No, I guess not," I said.

"So what's your problem?"

"Right now, it's getting a sunburn," I said. "My fair skin doesn't last long in this direct sun."

"Let's go swimming," Hilary suggested. "At least that will cool us off."

"Good idea," I said.

We paddled around in the pool and sighed about how good it felt. I stayed submerged as much as I could, but Hilary didn't want to get her hair wet.

"There's Candy talking to Travis," I reported to Hilary.

"Yeah, I see them," Hilary said. "I think they're older than we are."

"What gives you that idea?"

"They don't pay much attention to us."

Just then Candy and Travis got into the pool and asked us if we wanted to play catch with a beach ball.

"Sure," I said, grinning at Hilary.

We played around in the pool until my

sunburn hurt. Then Hilary and I went to change and explore the ship. Staying out of the sun was a must.

The elevators and corridors were cool and dark. We stopped on the Promenade Deck. "This level looks interesting. Let's check out the shops," I suggested.

We browsed through the clothes and jewelry in the boutique. Hilary had to buy two new bracelets to add to her collection. I decided I shouldn't tell her she had enough of them already.

Then we strolled through all the lounges. We even stuck our heads in the Teen Room for a bit.

"Uh, Niki," Hilary began, "what do you say we stop our tour here? I'd love to just rest and listen to music for a while."

"That's okay with me." We chose a table and sat down.

"Say, Hilary," I said, trying to be cool. "I just happened to notice something." I held up the Teen Room menu.

"Oh, yeah? What did you just happen to notice on the menu?" Hilary asked.

"Hot fudge sundaes."

"Sounds divine," Hilary said, closing her eyes.

The waiter came to take our order.

"I'll have a hot fudge sundae with the works—nuts, whipped cream, and a cherry on the top," I said.

"Don't put all that stuff on mine." Hilary made a face. "I want just plain vanilla ice cream and hot fudge, please."

While we were waiting for our sundaes, *Love Boat* came on the big screen TV.

I laughed. "My best friend, Jenny, told me this cruise would be like *Love Boat*," I confessed. "But it isn't anything like it."

"What do you mean?"

"We don't know the crew on a first name basis," I said. "No one is falling in love in front of our eyes."

"Oh, I don't know," Hilary said. "Isn't your grandmother falling in love with Tom?"

"Well, you may be right," I admitted. "I hadn't thought of that."

"And you like Darren," Hilary went on. "Do you think Travis is cute?"

"Kind of," I said. "He's not my type though."

"I go for big muscular guys," Hilary whispered. "I asked him if he played football and his whole face lit up."

The waiter brought our sundaes. Soon we were scraping the last taste of hot fudge out of the bottom of our sundae dishes. When the

TV show was over, we reluctantly decided to go get ready for dinner.

When I got back to my cabin, Isabel was putting on her diamond earrings. She was all dressed up in her beaded black dress.

"You look nice, ISABEL," I said, emphasizing her name.

"Thank you, Granddaughter," she said with a smile. "I like getting dressed up for dinner. Everyone puts on their special manners when they're dressed up, don't you think?"

"I guess so," I said. "I had a really good time with Hilary today."

"That's wonderful," Isabel said.

I headed for the shower. When I got out, I put on my scratchy pink dress. I hoped it didn't make too much noise when I walked.

Isabel smiled. "You look terrific, too, Niki. Let's go. We're off to the Captain's Gala Show."

I giggled. "Nobody could make the Captain's Gala Show sound as glamorous as you, Grandmother . . . I mean, Isabel."

First, we went to the cocktail party. We stood in line for twenty minutes just to shake hands with the Captain. If it had been up to me, I would have skipped that part.

Isabel met Tom in the line. They chattered on about bridge and other boring things that adults talk about. I wondered where Darren was.

After dinner we got a front row seat for the show. First, the cruise director introduced the Captain. Then he introduced a comedian in a tuxedo, who told jokes and did fascinating magic tricks.

I liked the comedian better than the singer who performed next. She had red hair and wore a red sequined dress. She sounded okay, but I felt like dancing instead of sitting.

I guess Isabel noticed I was restless. "Niki, dear, why don't you run along to the Teen Room whenever you want," she whispered to me during intermission. "After the show the band is going to play, and I'm sure you don't want to dance to OUR music." She looked at Tom meaningfully. He smiled at her.

"Okay," I said. I slipped out right before the singer started to perform again. One couple was already dancing.

I took a deep breath of the cool, fresh air. Then I heard a familiar voice behind me.

"I saw you leave, Niki. Are you going to the Teen Room?" It was Craig.

"Yes," I said. Somehow when I thought of dancing, I didn't think of Craig.

"That's a coincidence," Craig said, smiling. "That's where I'm going. That old fogey music was getting to me."

"Me, too," I admitted.

The elevator doors opened, and a couple got out who were speaking Spanish.

Craig and I looked at each other. When the doors closed, we said in unison, "Do you take Spanish?"

We giggled. "Yes, I take Spanish," I said. "And I thought about asking you that question this afternoon."

"So did I," Craig said.

We arrived at the Teen Room, giggling about how my dress rustled when I walked.

"You'll never get a job as a cat burglar in that dress, Niki," Craig said.

"I'll just have to think of another occupation."

I was smiling at Craig as we sat down. Then I noticed Darren at the other end of the table. Oh, no, I thought. What if Darren thinks I like Craig? That could ruin my chances with Darren for the rest of the cruise.

"Want to dance?" Craig asked.

"Sure." What could I say?

It was a fast song. I was surprised Craig was such a good dancer. And I was nervous because Darren was staring right at us.

Craig and I danced three dances in a row. After each one I thought sure Darren was going to ask me to dance. Each time though, Craig asked me first. My heart was pounding so loud, I thought I was going to collapse.

"Come on, Niki, we're getting good at this." Craig was dancing by himself next to the table.

"I need to rest," I said, wiping my forehead. I was sweating in my new pink dress.

"How about a cola?" Craig asked.

"Yeah, that sounds great," I said.

He went over to the refreshment bar. I tried to cool off and watch Darren without being obvious. Then my heart dropped 10,000 feet. Darren was walking toward me!

But Candy intercepted him and started talking to him. He smiled and seemed very glad to see her.

"Here you go, Niki." Craig handed me my cola.

"Thanks." I said. I was just sick. When were Darren and I ever going to get together?

We sat through the next dance, and Darren and Candy kept right on grinning at each other. Unlike me, Candy seemed to have plenty of things to talk to Darren about.

Then another fast song started. Darren was walking toward me again. My heart was doing a hard rock beat.

"Oh, Niki, come on. This is my favorite song." Before I knew what was happening,

Craig grabbed my hand and pulled me onto the dance floor. The last I saw of Darren, he was staring at us. I knew I was doomed.

Craig smiled at me as we danced. He was so much fun to dance with, I couldn't help smiling at him. The problem was, I knew how our grinning at each other must look to Darren. I had to do something fast.

When the song was over, I mumbled some excuse to Craig and rushed over to Hilary.

"Want to go for a walk on the deck?" I asked desperately. "It's too hot and noisy in here."

"Sure." Hilary followed me out of the double doors onto the deck. "What's up?"

"Hilary, you have to help me," I said in a rush. "I want to dance with Darren, but he'll never ask me as long as Craig asks me every dance. What am I going to do?"

"That's easy." Hilary blinked at me. "I'll ask Craig to dance."

"Oh, would you, Hilary? That would be so great of you."

"No problem," she said.

We marched back into the Teen Room. Hilary promptly asked Craig to dance. I sat down at the table and looked around for Darren, but I couldn't see him. Craig and Hilary appeared to be having a great time.

Craig seemed to like to dance no matter who his partner was.

I sipped my cola. Where was Darren? My heart started to pound again. Now that I had it all arranged, he had disappeared. Candy was gone, too. Travis was sitting at the table connecting drinking straws.

The song ended. I saw Hilary grab Craig's arm and talk to him at the edge of the dance floor. He glanced at me and then went on talking.

I didn't know what to do. Darren was still missing. A slow song started, and Hilary and Craig started dancing again. I looked at Travis, and he jumped up and mumbled something about the rest room.

When the dance was over, Craig left the room. Hilary came over and sat down.

"I tried to stall him as long as I could," she said.

"Thanks for trying," I said. "I guess Darren left."

"Well, we tried," Hilary said, looking around.

"Where did Craig go?" I asked.

"I don't know," Hilary answered. "He said something about practicing his backhand."

"What a night this is," I said.

"Let's go for a walk," Hilary said. "I can't

take anymore of the heat in here."

"Me either." We left during a slow song.

We hadn't gone more than twenty feet when we ran into Darren. Hilary gave me one of her stares, and I burst out laughing.

"What's so funny?" Darren asked.

"Oh, nothing," I said.

"Are you two going to enter a skit in the talent show?" Darren asked.

"What talent show?" Hilary asked.

"The Teen Room is sponsoring a talent show tomorrow night," Darren explained. "Candy told me all about it. There's a meeting about the skits tomorrow morning."

"Now that sounds like something I could get into," Hilary said.

"Yeah, it would be fun," I said. "Let's do a skit together, want to?"

"Definitely," Hilary said.

"I'll see you tomorrow," Darren said smiling.

"Right," I said, smiling back.

I said good night to Hilary and Darren and went to my cabin. Isabel wasn't back yet.

I decided to write a P.S. on my letter to Jenny. I told her about dancing with Craig instead of Darren. But I also wrote I was going to be in a skit with Hilary. And the best part, I told her, was that I would get to spend more time with Darren tomorrow.

Five

I was having breakfast with Tom and Isabel in the dining room and watching the blue-green sea rise and fall on the horizon.

"Isabel, I can't wait to show you San Juan," Tom said. "Not the Americanized part, but the Old City. We'll have the best meal of black beans and rice you've ever tasted."

"I can hardly wait," Isabel said, looking into his eyes.

You would have thought they were sixteen, the way they acted.

I noticed Craig was having breakfast with his parents. This morning he didn't wave or even look at me.

Actually, I was relieved Craig wasn't pestering me. I was too busy to talk to him. I was going to see Darren at the skit meeting.

Hilary came over to our table. "Ready to go, Niki?" she asked.

"Hello, Hilary," Isabel said. "Where are you two going so early this morning?"

"Hello, Mrs. Sloane," Hilary said. "Niki and I are practicing a skit for the talent show tonight."

"My, how energetic of you," Isabel said. "Don't let me keep you."

"Bye," I said. "I don't know if I'll be finished by lunch. I might eat in the Teen Room."

"That's fine, dear. Have a wonderful day." Isabel smiled at me and then at Tom. I had a feeling she was going to have a wonderful day without me.

Hilary and I started toward the elevator.

"My grandmother and Tom are beginning to act like real lovebirds," I said. "Did you see how she looked at him?"

"You look at Darren that way, too," Hilary said.

"I hope I'm not that bad," I said, getting on the elevator.

"Think about how we giggled when we saw Darren on the deck last night," Hilary said.

"I guess you're right," I admitted. "I hadn't thought of it in that way." The elevator doors opened, and we went to the Teen Room.

"Hello, everybody." Darren met us at the door. He seemed to be especially energetic today.

"Hi." I was all smiles.

"Good morning, Darren," Hilary said dramatically, but she looked excited, too.

"This is Sue," Darren said. "She's the coordinator of the talent show."

"Great!" Sue said, sizing us up. "More talent. Did you two girls—let's see, what are your names?"

We told her our names, and she wrote them down on her clipboard. "Did you have any particular skit in mind?"

Hilary and I looked at each other. "No," I said.

"How would you like to do a take off on the Cinderella story?" Sue asked.

"Marvelous," Hilary said. "I'll be the stepmother." She assumed a wicked step-mother pose. Immediately I knew she'd be fantastic.

"Hilary, I didn't know you liked acting," I said.

"Darling, there are lots of things you don't know about me," Hilary said, tossing her long, blond curls, and gesturing the length of the Teen Room.

"When Hilary gets through auditioning, Sue will tell you the rest of the instructions," Darren said, folding his arms. "No hurry, Hilary, the talent show isn't until tonight.

There's plenty of time." He grinned at her.

Hilary dropped her arms and glared good-naturedly at Darren.

"Niki, why don't you be Cinderella?" Sue asked.

"Okay," I said.

Sue wrote on her clipboard. "And Hilary is the stepmother." She smiled at Hilary. "Come on over here and I'll introduce you to the rest of your group."

We followed Sue to our group. Peter, a blond boy who was about ten, was my prince. Sheila and Nancy were the stepsisters. They looked about eleven.

"Now this is a Cinderella story with a twist," Sue said as she passed out the scripts. "Cinderella is definitely her own person with a good head on her shoulders. And the prince is a rather frightened sort, who is very content to have Cinderella fight the dragons for him. It's a marriage made in heaven." She laughed.

"It sounds like fun," I said to Hilary when Sue had gone on to another group.

"Let's check out the script," Hilary said. "Come on, group. I see a quiet place in the back of the room."

"What is this?" I teased. "Hilary, have you appointed yourself our director?"

"I've had the lead in our class plays for the

last three years," Hilary announced. "Besides, somebody has to do it."

"Okay," I said. "Come on, group. Listen to what the stepmother has to say."

With a nod at me Hilary took over. She was great at getting the little kids to learn their lines and ham it up at the same time.

I glanced over at Darren, who was the tin man in "The Wizard of Oz." Candy was Dorothy in Darren's group. I wished it could have been me instead. I didn't like the way she smiled at him.

We took a break from rehearsal for lunch. Hilary and I found a table in the back, separate from the little kids.

"Where did Darren go?" I asked, looking around. "I didn't see him leave."

"He must have gone out on deck," Hilary said, studying her cheeseburger.

"I don't see Candy either," I said crossly. "Did you see the way she was smiling at him?"

"Niki, any girl who looks at Darren is going to smile at him that way," Hilary said slowly as if she were explaining something to one of the little kids.

"That's nice," I said, plopping down my cheeseburger. "You aren't making me feel any better."

"I'm just facing facts," Hilary said. "But

don't worry. If he's really interested in you, he'll be back."

"I don't know," I said. "With Candy around and Craig always in the picture, he might forget about me altogether."

"My problem is how are we going to get Peter to look sixteen instead of ten," Hilary mused. Then she added, "Why don't you talk to Candy?"

"What do you mean?"

Hilary shrugged. "It never hurts to size up the competition. You might decide you have nothing to worry about."

"That's a good idea," I said. "Thanks, Hilary."

"Don't mention it," she said. "But you can't talk to her now. We have to get back to work."

The afternoon seemed to fly by. Finally, when Hilary thought our skit was ready, she dismissed us to go dress for dinner. I had been watching Candy all afternoon, but I'd never found a chance to talk to her.

"Oh, I'm sorry," I said. I nearly bumped into Candy as I was coming out of the Teen Room.

"I'll see you later, Niki." Hilary gave me one of her do-it-now-or-else looks and left.

"That's all right," Candy said, smiling. "I was standing in the doorway."

"How's your skit coming?" I asked.

"I think it's going to be good," Candy answered. "Our scarecrow is a little weak, but then he's supposed to look scared, right?" She laughed.

I smiled. "Yeah, nobody will notice."

"And your skit? Are you pleased with it?" Candy asked.

"I think so, if the little kids don't freeze up on us . . . and if we can get Peter to stop giggling," I said. Candy was really nice. I liked her in spite of the fact that she smiled at Darren all the time.

"Maybe you could pinch Peter right before you go on stage or something," Candy said, laughing.

"Good idea." I giggled.

"I'll see you later," Candy said. "I'd better go get ready. We have the first sitting at dinner."

"Bye," I said. Why does she have to be nice? I wondered. In the back of my mind, I was sure she meant trouble where Darren was concerned.

On the way to my cabin, I met Craig in the hall.

"Hey, how's it going?" Craig asked. "I haven't seen you all day."

"Fine, how are you?" I realized I looked a wreck.

"Want to go dancing in the Rendezvous Lounge after dinner?" Craig asked. "I hear they have a terrific rock band."

"I'd like to, but I can't," I said. "There's a talent show competition in the Teen Room, and I'm Cinderella." Saying that made me laugh. "No, really. I've been practicing all day for this Cinderella skit."

"Well, I guess the band will be there all week," Craig said. "Good luck tonight."

"Thanks, we'll need it."

* * * * *

Later in the dining room, Isabel chattered to Tom all through dinner, but I hardly heard her. For once, I didn't have an appetite. I skipped dessert and met up with Hilary in the rest room on the Promenade Deck.

We told each other how nervous we were and hurried toward the Teen Room. Sue was already handing out the costumes.

"Now here's the order of the skits," Sue shouted over the confusion. "First, 'Wizard of Oz,' second, 'Johnny Apple Cider,' third, 'Star Fights,' and last but not least, 'Cinderella.' "

"We're last. I'll never make it," Hilary groaned. "I'm half sick now."

"You'll make it, Hilary," I said.

"First skit cast be backstage at least ten minutes before showtime," Sue requested. "Any questions?"

"Do you have any antacids?" Hilary asked.

Sue smiled and put her arm around Hilary. "A few butterflies never hurt anyone," she said.

Darren's group was first. They were definitely funny. Candy was a dingbat Dorothy, who kept forgetting why they were on the yellow-brick road.

Darren was a heartless tin man, who somehow got the cowardly lion's roar. The wizard was a computer programmer, who was afraid of people. The audience loved it.

Hilary and I were sitting in the audience during the applause. I looked at her with alarm.

"Don't worry," Hilary whispered. "We'll be better."

"I hope so," I said.

During the third skit my stomach started doing flip-flops. "Oh, no," I said.

"What's the matter?" Hilary whispered.

"Craig just came in." I nodded toward the door.

"So?" Hilary was trying to watch the action on stage.

"I don't want Craig to keep me from Darren

again tonight," I said. "I already have to worry about Candy."

"Forget it," Hilary advised. "Craig isn't dancing tonight." She smiled mysteriously.

I wondered what that meant, but the skit was over.

"We're on next," Hilary said during the applause. "Come on, Niki." She rounded up the little kids and headed backstage.

I glanced at Craig. He waved and smiled. I smiled at him and went backstage. I was too nervous to think.

"Okay, places everybody," Hilary commanded in a stage whisper.

We rushed to our places, and the curtain rose.

As the stepmother, Hilary had the first lines. She was so good, a hush came over the audience. The rest of us tried our best to give a good performance just to keep up with her. Peter didn't giggle once.

I really got into the Cinderella part. I was having fun no matter what the audience thought. But they must have liked us. When the skit was over, they went crazy with applause.

"I think that's more applause than anybody else got," I whispered, peering through the curtains.

"I think so, too," Hilary said. We hugged each other excitedly.

Sue came on the stage and directed the audience to vote for their favorite skit with their applause. "The Wizard of Oz" got a lot of applause. Darren and his cast took two curtain calls.

Hilary made a doubtful face at me. I shook my head and gave her the thumbs-up sign.

"Johnny Apple Cider" and "Star Fights" each got less applause. Then we went to take our bow. Sue said, "Cinderella," and the audience went crazy again. We had three curtain calls!

"The winner is . . . 'Cinderella,'" Sue shouted. We went up to accept our prize, a record for each of us.

I went to return my costume to Sue. Hilary followed me backstage.

"Niki, did you watch Craig during the judging of applause?" she asked.

"No, why?"

"Craig was leading the applause for our skit."

"What do you mean?"

"He was standing at the side, clapping and whistling and motioning for the crowd to applaud more," Hilary whispered.

"He was? Do you think that's why we won?"

"No, I think we were the best," Hilary said, smiling. "But it was nice of Craig to cheer for us."

"Yes, it was nice," I agreed, putting my Cinderella skirt in the trunk.

When I emerged from behind the curtain, Craig was standing there.

"Oh, hi, Craig," I said, looking around for Darren.

"Hi, Niki," Craig said. "I really liked your skit."

"Thanks," I said.

Then Darren came up to me. "Hi, Cinderella," he said. "Want to walk on the deck for a while?"

"Okay," I said, looking back over my shoulder. Craig was standing there alone watching me leave.

Six

AS Darren and I walked out on the deck, the sea breeze cooled my face.

"I didn't realize how warm it was in there," I said.

"I'm still sweating from the skits," Darren said. "Let's stand over by the railing and cool off."

"Yeah, that's a good idea."

"It's amazing how steady this ship stays in the middle of the ocean," Darren said, leaning against the railing. "I almost forgot where I was while we were doing the skits."

"So did I now that you mention it."

"Your skit was really good, Niki."

"Thanks," I said, smiling. "I liked yours, too."

"You know, I was thinking," Darren said. "Whenever I'm with you, we always talk about me. Let's talk about you for a change."

"Me?" My mind went blank. "There's not much to say about me." As hard as I tried, I couldn't think of a single interesting thing to say about myself.

Fortunately Hilary saved me.

"Sorry to interrupt," she said. "But do you think I could tag along with you and your grandmother to San Juan tomorrow? My parents are going on a boring tour, and I don't want to go."

"Sure, I'd love it," I said. "Isabel and Tom will be together. With you along I'll have someone to talk to."

"Thanks, Niki," Hilary said. "I'll meet you in the morning after breakfast. Night."

"Night, Hilary," I said.

"See you tomorrow," Darren added.

When Hilary had gone, I turned to Darren. "Hilary and I have become pretty good friends considering I only met her a few days ago."

"She's really nice," Darren said. "Whose this Craig guy anyway? He thinks he's a pretty good friend of yours, too."

"He's very nice, really," I said. "He tries to be friendly, only sometimes he acts a little weird."

"He sure wanted your skit to win."

"He was only trying to help," I said.

"I felt like telling him off," Darren said.

I wondered if Darren was mad about Craig's hanging around me or that his skit lost the competition. "Would you like to take our walk around the deck now?" I asked.

Darren sighed. "I guess so."

We walked the length of the deck, not saying a word. Then Darren said, "It is getting late." He walked me to my cabin and left quickly.

I was depressed. I went inside and wrote a letter to Jenny. I told her about the skits and walking on the deck with Darren. I left out Darren's nasty attitude.

* * * * *

The next morning I couldn't wait to talk to Hilary. I found her after breakfast while we were waiting for the launch to take us to San Juan.

"Hilary, I need your advice," I began.

"What major catastrophe have you gotten yourself into this time?" Hilary asked with a grin.

I told her about last night. "Craig was disappointed because I left with Darren, and Darren acted jealous of Craig. What am I going to do?"

"The best thing is to do nothing. You worry

too much, Niki," Hilary said, waving an arm of chunky bracelets at me. "Forget about it for a while."

"Maybe you're right," I said. I saw Isabel and Tom approaching. "Let's go to San Juan and have a great time."

"Now you're talking," Hilary said enthusiastically.

"Niki and Hilary, it's time to go ashore," Isabel called. "Hilary, I'm so glad you could come with us today, dear. I'm sure Niki will appreciate your company."

"Thank you for having me," Hilary said, smiling.

The four of us went to the loading area and climbed aboard the dinghy. After a short, bumpy ride, we scrambled out and tried our wobbly sea legs on dry land.

"I feel as if I'm still on the ship," Isabel exclaimed.

"It's amazing what a few days at sea does to your sense of balance," Tom observed.

"The salt spray has ruined my hair," Hilary said.

Tom arranged for a taxi ride around the island with the driver as our tour guide.

"Look, Niki, there's El Morro Castle," Isabel exclaimed.

"Wow, that's impressive," I said. The golden

castle was built on a high cliff that jutted out over the ocean. Our driver said it was built there so the original inhabitants could see an enemy approaching from any direction.

We got out of the taxi to tour the inside of the castle.

"This place is amazing," Hilary said, as we trudged through the dank corridors.

"It's spooky in a way," I said. "I feel like a pirate is going to jump out at me every time we turn down one of these winding passageways."

I think both of us were relieved when we emerged into the sunshine again. I thought about Cinderella.

"You sure were a great stepmother," I said to Hilary.

"Thanks," Hilary said, smiling. "What made you think about the skit?"

"Cinderella lived in a castle," I said, motioning to the castle behind us.

Hilary laughed. "You were a great Cinderella, too."

"Thank you," I said.

"Now all we have to do is find your grandmother," Hilary noted.

"No problem," I said. "She'll be in the gift shop."

"How do you know?" Hilary asked.

"Just follow me," I said.

We followed the signs to the gift shop. Sure enough, there was Isabel buying booklets and postcards.

"I know I shouldn't buy all this stuff," she kept saying.

Hilary and I smiled at each other. I bought a miniature knight for my brother Jimmy. Of course, Hilary had to buy a bracelet with a Spanish design on it.

When we got back in the taxi, Tom asked the driver to take us to a good place for lunch. He drove us to the Old City to a restaurant known for its black beans and rice.

"Isn't this quaint?" Isabel exclaimed, when we had been seated.

The restaurant had a golden tile floor, sort of the same color as the stone of El Morro Castle. In the center of the main room was a fountain with a stained glass skylight above it. Guitar music played softly in the background.

"Tropical fruit punch for everyone," Tom said in an excited voice.

"Oh, Tom, this place is so lovely." Isabel got tears in her eyes.

"It's beautiful," I said.

Hilary was watching a cute waiter with a thin black moustache. He brought a pottery pitcher of punch and four glasses. He poured a glass and set it in front of me. Then he clicked his heels together and bowed slightly. I smiled and felt my face grow warm. He did the same thing for Hilary, Isabel, and Tom. We all giggled.

"To three lovely ladies," Tom said, raising his glass.

"To the *Sun Goddess*, and new friendships," Isabel said, clinking her glass to Tom's.

We ordered black beans and rice. The waiter bowed again and disappeared.

"Did you notice how cute the waiter is?" Hilary whispered, glancing at Isabel. She and Tom were talking about the old days.

"Yeah, maybe he could get a job on the ship," I whispered back.

The food was delicious. Some marvelous dark bread and a great salad came with the meal. I think I ate half a loaf of the bread. I asked for more just to see the waiter click his heels and bow once more.

"Oh, I ate too much," I groaned.

"So did I," Isabel said. "It was so delicious."

Hilary ate her usual three bites. She never ate very much. "I guess I ate too much breakfast," she said.

After lunch Tom paid the taxi driver and we walked around the Old San Juan. By the end of the afternoon, Hilary and I decided we had seen enough old buildings for one day.

Finally we said good-bye to Isabel and Tom. They were going on a night club tour of San Juan. Then Hilary and I took the dinghy back to the ship. It was Teen Night in the disco, and we were excited about it.

* * * * *

In the hall outside my door, I ran into Craig. I wondered if he had been waiting for me.

"Did you have a good time in San Juan?" Craig asked.

"It was wonderful," I said. "San Juan's a beautiful city."

"I like it, too," Craig agreed, "especially El Morro Castle."

"We went there, too."

"I bought my brother a knight," Craig said.

I laughed. "You'll never guess what I bought my brother."

"Oh, yes, I would." Craig smiled. "Are you going to Teen Night in the disco?"

"Yes," I said. "I have to get ready though."

"Great. Why don't I meet you there later?"

"Okay." I said good-bye and unlocked the cabin door.

First I wrote a letter to Jenny. I had a hard time describing San Juan. I finally told her she'd have to go there herself to see how pretty it was.

Then the phone rang. It was Darren. "Are you going to the disco?" he asked.

"Yes, but I'm not ready yet," I answered.

"I'll see you there," he said and hung up.

Oh, no, I thought. What a night this was going to be. Trying to be with Darren and having Craig hanging around would be definitely difficult.

A few minutes later I walked into the disco and saw Craig waving at me. Hilary was sitting with him. The disco was decorated in black and silver and had a revolving mirrored ball suspended from the ceiling. Rock music blared on the stereo system.

"I'm sorry, but this is the best table I could get," Craig said.

"This must be a popular event," I said, sitting down at the crowded table. I looked around. Darren hadn't shown up yet.

"Kids like to wear jeans and really dance, not just shuffle around in fancy clothes," Hilary declared.

"Come on, Niki, let's dance." Craig was having a hard time sitting still.

It was early, so only four other couples were dancing. Whatever outrageous step Craig did, I followed.

I had thought I was tired from walking around San Juan all day. But we danced and danced. When we finally stopped to eat, everyone clapped for us.

"What's on the menu?" Craig asked. "I'm starved."

"I thought you were going to dance all night," Hilary said.

"I will, but after I eat," Craig said, smiling.

The menu consisted of hamburgers or pizza. We all ordered hamburgers and fries.

After we ate, the band started playing again. Travis asked Hilary to dance. She looked pleased. Craig pulled me out onto the dance floor again. His feet hardly touched the floor.

Craig loved dancing better than any guy I'd ever known. I had so much fun dancing with him, I almost forgot to look for Darren. Then, toward the end of the evening, I saw him.

"Hilary, don't look now, but guess who's dancing with Candy?" I whispered, when Craig went to get more colas.

"I can't imagine." Hilary turned around and stared right at Darren. He smiled and nodded at us.

"I told you not to look," I groaned.

"Don't worry about it," Hilary said. "There are no rules that a guy can't dance with more than one girl."

"Well, why did he bother to call me if he planned to be with Candy?" I asked.

"Maybe he's going to dance with you next."

Craig came back with the colas, and the band announced they were quitting for the night.

"Oh, no," Craig moaned. "I was just warming up."

"I think my feet are warming down," I said, laughing.

"Come on, I'll walk you two to your cabins," Craig said. Travis had disappeared, and since Darren was with Candy, we both agreed.

"Ah, the fresh air feels good," Hilary said as we exited through the double doors. "It was really hot in there."

I was afraid to open my mouth. Darren and Candy came out right after us. Travis suddenly reappeared behind us and joined Hilary.

"Wouldn't it be nice to have something like the Teen Room back home, Darren?" Candy asked.

"Yeah, it's a fun place," Darren agreed.

"Are you from Daytona Beach, too?" Hilary asked Candy, surprised.

"Sure," Candy answered. "My parents and Darren's parents are best friends. They came on this cruise together."

"We go to the same high school," Darren added. "I thought you knew."

"I knew that!" Travis said, somewhat comically.

We all laughed.

Well, that explains a lot, I thought. As we reached the elevators, Candy started a round of good-byes. Then our group broke up to go to different floors.

"Good night, Cinderella," Craig said when we reached our hall. He smiled at me and left.

Darren had called me Cinderella, too. But somehow Craig had said it nicer. I didn't know what to think, especially now that I knew why Candy and Darren were always so friendly.

Seven

THE next morning after breakfast Isabel dragged me to a snorkeling and SCUBA lecture. I wanted to go swimming, but Isabel said I might as well take advantage of all the things the ship had to offer.

Well, at least the guy giving the lecture was good looking. And I was amazed. What he had to say was really very interesting. SCUBA sounded like a sport I could really get into.

"You run along and put on your swimming suit," Isabel said after the lecture. "I'll sit here in the sun for a while."

It seemed to take forever, waiting for elevators. I hurried to our cabin and changed into my suit. On the way back I ran into Hilary.

"Where have you been hiding?" Hilary asked.

"I went to a SCUBA lecture with Isabel," I

said. "Want to go swimming?"

"What a marvelous idea," Hilary said. She was already wearing her suit and carrying one of her books.

We made our way to the Lido Deck and found a couple lounge chairs. I dived into the pool as soon as we put our stuff down. The water was cool and refreshing. As usual Hilary was still standing on the steps.

"Come on in, the water is fine," I teased.

"If you don't mind, I like to do this gradually," Hilary answered.

I tried to swim some laps, but there were too many people in the pool. Hilary and I paddled around for a while.

"Oh, no," I said. "There's Darren. He sees us."

Hilary looked across the pool. "What's wrong with him seeing us?"

"My hair is a mess," I complained.

"I'm sure he's used to seeing girls with wet hair while they're swimming," Hilary said.

"Well, it's too late now anyway," I said.

Just then Darren dived into the pool and swam over to the side where we were.

"Hi, Darren," I said.

"Hey, this water feels great," he said. "Too bad you can't surf in it."

"Sorry about that," Hilary said.

"Will you settle for swimming laps instead?" I asked.

"You're on," Darren said, diving in and racing me to the other side. Of course he won.

"I gave you a head start," I said. Then I had to race him again with Hilary as the official starter.

When we had exhausted ourselves and driven all the adults out of the pool, Darren asked, "Why don't you two have lunch with me?"

"Sorry, I told my parents I'd meet them for lunch," Hilary said. "They seem to think they're not seeing enough of me on this cruise."

"Niki, how about you?" Darren asked, smiling at me.

"I'd like that."

Hilary got out of the pool. "I'll see you later," she said and left to find her parents.

I scrambled out and found my towel. "I'll tell Isabel our plans," I said to Darren. "Where shall we meet?"

"I'll meet you in the dining room," he said.

"Okay, I'll see you there."

"Oh, Niki, want to play tennis after lunch?" Darren asked.

I nodded, spoke to Isabel, and left. As usual, the elevator seemed to take forever. In the back of my mind, I still worried that Darren might not be waiting for me in the dining room.

I showered off as quickly as I could and raced back to the dining room. My stomach calmed a little when I saw Darren at a table by the window.

"That was a quick change," he said, rising to pull out my chair.

"I didn't even take time to dry my hair," I said, shaking my wet head.

"The sun will dry it quickly," Darren said. "Besides you look like a mermaid."

My heart beat faster. Nobody had called me a mermaid before. "I'm starved, aren't you?"

Then I was mad at myself for changing the subject. I never knew what to say when a boy flirted with me.

Darren studied the menu. "Yes, I am starved. I didn't realize it until I saw the menu."

We ordered bacon, lettuce, and tomato sandwiches. While we were waiting for our food, I told Darren about the SCUBA and snorkeling lecture.

"I've always wanted to take SCUBA lessons," Darren said. "Maybe I'll do it next summer. Too bad we can't take lessons together." He smiled.

"That would be fun," I said, my heart beating double time. "SCUBA might take time away from your surfing though."

"I doubt it," Darren said. "Besides I love any sport connected with the water."

Our sandwiches came. We munched on them and talked. Darren talked on and on about surfing.

"What's your favorite color?" I asked, impulsively.

Darren looked at me as if I'd said I saw a Martian. "I don't know, I like lots of colors. Why?"

"I just wondered," I said. I didn't seem to be able to make the questions a game like Craig did.

After lunch we put in our names for the tennis court and then stood around and waited. Finally it was our turn.

Darren was as good on the tennis court as I knew he must be at surfing. I'm afraid I spent more time watching him than I did playing tennis. He beat me five out of six games.

"I give up," I said, collapsing on the lounge chair at the end of the court.

"Your game must be off today," Darren said, smiling.

"I'm finding it hard to concentrate. Maybe it's the wind." I smiled at him.

We sat and watched the waves for a while. Darren kept pointing out the best ones for surfing.

"What's your favorite subject in school?" I asked.

"I like them all about the same, I guess," Darren said. He tossed his tennis racket from hand to hand and stopped talking.

This isn't the way it's supposed to work, I thought. I wished Darren would start talking about surfing again. Anything was better than silence.

"Do you like to play cards?" I asked. "I saw some kids playing Crazy Eights in the Teen Room the other day."

"I'm not much of a card player," Darren said, looking at his watch. "Wow, it's getting late. It's time to dress for dinner. I'll see you later, Niki, okay?"

I was so disappointed, I was speechless. I nodded at him, and he rushed toward the stairs. Well, Niki, you've charmed him again, I told myself. I picked up my racket and headed for my cabin. I felt like smashing a hundred tennis balls right off the stern of the ship.

As I fumbled with the key to my cabin door, the words of a letter to Jenny ran through my mind. I could hear Isabel in the shower as I entered the room. I got out the stationery and a pen and sat down to write.

Dear Jenny,

I had the best afternoon with Darren today. He called me a "mermaid" after watching me swim in the pool. He took me to lunch and entertained me with some of his surfing stories.

Then we played a divine set of tennis. I wore that white tennis outfit that makes my legs look skinny. I'm so tan now, I look even thinner. This afternoon was so dreamy I can imagine how wonderful tonight is going to be.

Well, I have to get ready for dinner now. Having a boyfriend keeps me so busy, I don't have time to do much except enjoy myself.

So long for now,

Niki

I read the letter, smiling to myself. It was perfect. I had told Jenny only the good things. I didn't mention the fact that Darren and I had nothing at all to talk about. But what vacation postcard ever told the bad things?

"What are you going to wear tonight, Niki?" Isabel asked as she emerged from the bathroom.

"I don't know," I said. "What do you think of this blue dress?" It was the one I had worn for eighth-grade graduation.

"It will be marvelous with your tan," Isabel said.

"You don't think it's too fancy, do you?" I asked.

"Not at all, Niki. I think it looks lovely on you." Isabel gave me a hug.

"You look pretty tonight," I told her. She was wearing a rose dress that made her skin glow.

"Thank you," she said. "Now hurry and get ready."

* * * * *

Strolling violinists played romantic music in the dining room. Tonight's dinner had a Greek theme.

"There he is. There's Tom," Isabel said, excitedly. She waved at him as we wove our way across the crowded dining room.

"My, how lovely you look, Isabel," Tom said when we reached his table.

"I told her she should wear that color all the time."

"How right you are, Niki," Tom said.

We sat down and looked over the menu. Fortunately all the Greek dishes were translated. Otherwise I wouldn't have known what to order. I finally decided on a Greek salad with Feta cheese, a lamb dish, and mousaka, a Greek noodle dish.

When dinner was finally over, I raced down to the Teen Room. I wondered if Darren would still be mad at me.

As I got out of the elevator, I saw Hilary and Craig walking together toward the Teen Room. I had a horrible sinking feeling.

Hilary and Craig did have the same dinner sitting as I did, I told myself. Anyway I wasn't interested in Craig. I liked Darren. Then why did I have such a bad feeling?

I started to catch up with them and ask what was going on. But something stopped me. I like Darren. So why am I worried about Hilary and Craig? I wondered. Do I like Craig, too? No, it couldn't be.

"Hey, Niki," Darren called as I entered the Teen Room.

"Hi," I said.

Darren smiled that wonderful smile and asked me to dance.

I noticed Hilary and Craig were dancing. They seemed to be having a good time. When the dance was over, they sat at a table by themselves. I looked for Travis, but I didn't see him.

Darren and I danced some more. He didn't say anything about leaving so abruptly after we played tennis. Over Darren's shoulder I noticed Hilary dancing with Craig again. Why should I care? I asked myself. I was dancing with Darren. What did it matter who danced with Craig? I must have asked myself that question two hundred times.

"Want to go to the movie at eleven?" Darren asked when the song was over.

"Sure," I said. "What's playing?"

"I don't know," Darren said. "Something romantic...."

I felt myself blush. I wondered how old you had to be before you stopped blushing when a guy said, "something romantic."

I excused myself to go to the rest room. Hilary was there combing her hair.

"Hey, Hilary, how's it going?" I tried to be cool.

"Fine, Niki," Hilary said. "You finally got the boy you wanted, didn't you?"

"Darren? Oh, yes, of course, Darren." I laughed. "Yeah, he's great."

"Craig is really turning out to be a blast," Hilary went on. "He's such a good dancer. And he's so funny. He's kept me laughing the whole evening."

"He is very funny," I said, my heart sinking again.

"See you tomorrow," Hilary said.

I walked slowly back to Darren. "What's the matter?" he asked. "Why the frown?"

"I don't know," I said, truthfully. "Is it time to go to the movie?"

"Yes, I think it is," he said, checking his watch.

We walked around the deck first—for the fresh air, Darren said. I hoped he wouldn't point out the surfing waves tonight.

Finally we got to the movie. Darren held my hand. Then I knew I was going crazy. Here I was in a romantic movie holding hands with a cute boy. And all I did was worry about Hilary dancing with a nerd named Craig!

Eight

ISABEL was tapping her foot and waiting for me to finish my breakfast. I could see she was anxious to explore St. Thomas. And knowing my grandmother, that meant shopping.

"Well, Niki," Isabel said, "we only have one day to see St. Thomas. What are we going to do with it?"

"We could lie on the world famous beaches," I teased.

"Or we could spend the day exploring the world famous shops," Isabel teased me back.

"Why don't we compromise?" I suggested. "We'll shop in the morning and swim in the afternoon when we're hot and tired."

"A marvelous idea," Isabel exclaimed. "What a diplomat you're becoming, Niki." She smiled at me.

"Did I hear someone mention world famous

shops and beaches?" Craig asked, slipping into the chair opposite mine.

"I guess you did," I said.

"How are you, Craig?" Isabel asked.

"I'm all ready for the fabulous bargains on St. Thomas," Craig said. "It has more jewelry stores per square foot than anywhere in the world."

"Jewelry stores?" Isabel blinked.

"You can get some really good buys on jewelry," Craig went on. He leaned forward intently.

"How do you know so much?" Isabel asked.

"My father's in the wholesale jewelry business," Craig explained. "He supplies some of the St. Thomas stores."

"Then you go on cruises all the time," I said, half to myself.

"No, not really. Most of the time we fly down here."

"I have an idea." Isabel looked inspired. "Why don't you come along with us, Craig? You can be our 'expert advisor' in the art of shopping."

"I'd love to," Craig said. "It's a lot of fun showing the shops to someone whose never been here before."

"Good. Then it's all settled." Isabel smiled, looked at me, and immediately frowned. I could tell by the look on her face, she wished she'd consulted me before inviting Craig.

I smiled at her and shrugged. "Having a guide will make shopping less boring."

"Great," Craig said. "I'll meet you on the Promenade Deck in, say, twenty minutes?"

"Fine," Isabel said. "I'll go get my purse."

"Wait a minute," Craig said. "I have a feeling I know something all three of us have in common."

I laughed, remembering his game of figuring out our likes and dislikes. "What could the three of us have in common?"

"I'll bet none of us is going to take a camera to St. Thomas," he said. "Come on, you can tell me. Am I right?"

I looked at Isabel. "Should we tell him?"

"Tell him what?" Isabel asked.

"That you're a professional photographer," I said, smothering a giggle.

Isabel burst into laughter. "You go ahead and tell him that if you wish," she said. "But it would be an out-and-out lie."

"What did I tell you?" Craig said, holding up his hands. "I'm on a roll today."

We laughed and went to our cabins. Craig had completely charmed Isabel. I couldn't believe it. We were both rushing to the Promenade Deck to be with Craig again. I had to admit I was still confused about last night.

* * * * *

We finally got to St. Thomas. I thought Isabel was going to have a heart attack trying to decide which of the little shops to go to first.

"Wooden salad bowls are very big here in St. Thomas," Craig said. "But let me guess." He put his hands over his eyes. "You two are not the wooden salad bowl type. You like stoneware bowls that go in the dishwasher."

Isabel and I laughed. "Right again," Isabel said.

"Don't tell him, he'll get even more conceited," I said.

Craig pretended he was going to punch my arm, and ended up holding my hand for a second.

We wandered in and out of several stores. Craig kept telling me little facts about the retail business. I kept telling him he knew a lot about selling.

Later, I noticed an ice cream shop across the street. "I'm melting from the heat. . . ." I began, looking longingly at the store.

"Don't say it," Craig said, holding up his hand. "Three hot fudge sundaes coming up."

100

"Now, how did he know that?" Isabel exclaimed.

"I already told him I love hot fudge sundaes," I confessed.

"Thank goodness. I was beginning to think this young man was endowed with ESP."

We entered the cool ice cream shop with its red and white striped chairs and tables.

"We'll have three hot fudge sundaes," Craig said to the waiter.

Isabel and I drank our ice water and rested. Craig kept right on talking about St. Thomas.

"Next, we'll go to my uncle's jewelry store," he said. "It's not far from here."

"We shouldn't be having this," Isabel said as the waiter set her sundae in front of her. "You know we're meeting Tom for lunch."

"We'll worry about that at lunch," Craig said, attacking his sundae.

I began to eat. With me a hot fudge sundae is serious business.

After the ice cream break Isabel got serious about shopping. She bought a string of pearls from Craig's uncle. Both Craig and his uncle assured her they were a good buy.

"You must keep these pearls a secret, Niki," Isabel said. "They're for your mother. Her birthday is next month."

"I won't tell," I promised.

Isabel bought a sapphire ring for herself, exclaiming at the same time how extravagant she was being. Then she insisted on buying me a pearl ring. Craig assured her she was buying everything at the best possible prices.

We left the jewelry store and headed for the restaurant to meet Tom. He had a table waiting for us when we got there.

"Oh, Tom, you'll never guess what I did," Isabel began. Then we had to unwrap everything and show him.

"It looks like you've had a great shopping trip," Tom said, chuckling.

"Oh, it was marvelous," Isabel told him. "I had intended to buy some jewelry anyway. Having Craig to advise me was a bonus I hadn't counted on. Thank you so much, Craig."

"Hey, I enjoyed it," Craig protested.

"I hadn't realized how much of a science retailing is," I said, picking up my menu. "And I think I'll have iced tea for lunch."

"Can you believe it? That's just what I was going to order," Craig said.

Isabel laughed. "That's another thing you and Craig have in common," she said.

Isabel ended up ordering a shrimp dish, and Craig and I split another shrimp order. Tom ordered a big lobster meal, because he hadn't had a hot fudge sundae, he said.

Then Tom and Craig got into a conversation about deep sea fishing. I wondered if there was anything about the islands Craig didn't know.

When Tom ordered coffee after lunch, I was disappointed. I knew we had to be back to the ship by six o'clock. And I wanted to spend as much time on the beach as possible.

Even though I had been cruising on the ocean for the last five days, I missed the beach. I longed to dig my toes into the sand.

Finally Tom hailed a taxi. The driver took us to Magens Bay, the most famous beach on the island.

I was really excited about the prospect of seeing one of the most beautiful beaches in the world. It seemed to take forever for the rattling taxi to climb the winding road.

When we first got there, the bath house seemed a little primitive. We changed into our suits as soon as possible and left the bath house behind.

"I can actually see my toes, the water is so clear," I said, wading up to my neck.

"This area is famous for its clear water," Craig said, smiling at me.

"It's like a warm, salt-water bath," Isabel exclaimed.

"I'm not much of a beach person," Tom said. "But this water is certainly refreshing."

Since we were in a bay, there were no waves at all. The clear water barely lapped against the white sand beach.

Craig swam out about twenty-five yards. He stood up and waved. "Come on out, Niki. The water is fine."

I laughed. The bay was so shallow, you could swim straight out and still stand on the bottom. I swam out to where Craig was and waved at Isabel and Tom.

"I love Magens Bay," I said.

"I usually hitchhike out here when I'm staying with my uncle," Craig said. "So I guess that means I love it, too."

"Really?" I said. "That's one more thing we have in common."

"That's two more things," Craig said, smiling.

"What's the other one?" I asked.

"You're playing my what-do-we-have-in-common game."

"I guess you're right." Suddenly I splashed water in his face.

"Hey, what'd you do that for?" he asked, wiping his face. He splashed me back and dived in, swimming toward shore. I swam after him. We played around in the clear water for a while. Then when we got tired, we sat on our towels on the beach.

"The sticky, hot feeling I had this morning is all gone," I said.

"I feel great, too," Craig agreed.

"It's like the shopping trip happened a long time ago," I said. I was silent a minute. "I wonder if this cruise will seem like a dream that happened a long time ago once I get back home?"

"If it does, you'll have to come back," Craig said.

"I think you're right."

Then Isabel called to us to change for the ride back to the dock. We were all feeling very relaxed, so nobody said much on the way. We soaked up the scenic green hills behind the winding road.

Tom and Craig talked some more about fishing. I couldn't wait to get back to the ship and write to Jenny.

Nine

"THE masquerade ball is tonight," Isabel said when we reached our cabin. "I don't know whether to be happy or sad. It's our last night on the ship."

"This week has gone by so fast," I admitted.

"I need to wash off the salt from the ocean," Isabel said. "Then I can think about putting on my costume."

"You can take the first shower," I offered. I was thinking about what a perfect day we'd had in St. Thomas. I hadn't wanted to leave the beach and come back to the ship.

"Thank you, Niki," she said. "I'll rest a minute first."

I lay on my bed composing a letter to Jenny in my mind. When Isabel went in the bathroom, I got out my stationery.

Dear Jenny,

Today was even more wonderful than yesterday. Darren, Isabel, and I went to St. Thomas. Darren's uncle owns a jewelry shop on the island. Can you believe it? Isabel actually bought me a pearl ring.

The best part came later. Darren and I swam and lay on the beach all afternoon. It was heavenly.

I can't wait to show you my ring and my tan.

So long for now,

Niki

I read the letter and frowned. I hadn't left anything out this time. I had only changed one little name. I didn't know why I lied to Jenny. I guess somehow the story seemed more romantic with Darren rather than Craig.

I put the letter away quickly when Isabel came out of the bathroom.

"Tonight is going to be so much fun, Niki," Isabel said. "Dressing up in a costume makes me feel mysterious."

"I think it'll be fun, too," I said.

I took a long shower and thought about Darren and Craig. I guess what I wanted to do was take a little from each of them and make a perfect guy. When you think about it, what girl doesn't want to do that?

When I came out of the bathroom, I laughed at Isabel. She was dressed in green from her pointed cap to her little pointed boots. The costume made her look even tinier than she really was.

"How do I look?" she asked, turning around. "I'm Peter Pan."

"And Tom is going to be...?"

"Captain Hook, who else?" Isabel said, laughing.

"Who else?" I repeated, trying not to laugh. Isabel looked so excited. I expected her to take off and fly around the cabin at any minute.

"I can't wait any longer," Isabel said. "I have to show Tom. Why don't I meet you in the dining room?"

"Okay," I said, watching my grandmother glide out of the room.

We had rented our costumes from the ship's store. I was going as an ordinary pirate. My costume included black pants and a billowing white shirt. I'd bought a red scarf and a huge black moustache to go with the outfit.

I put on the pants and shirt, then tied the scarf around my neck. No, that won't do. I look like a Boy Scout, I thought.

Next, I tied the red scarf around my head like I'd seen in the old pirate movies on TV. I slapped on my moustache and studied my reflection in the mirror. "Now I'm getting closer to an authentic pirate," I said to myself. I giggled all the way to the dining room.

I could hardly keep from laughing when I met Hilary at the door. She was wearing purple pants, orange suspenders, a lavendar shirt, and a short black beard.

"Niki, a moustache becomes you," Hilary said, smiling.

"I love you in a beard, Hilary," I said, laughing. "Wait until you see my grandmother. And Tom should be even funnier."

"I've seen them," Hilary said. "They're marvelous. Want to eat together?"

"Good idea." I went over to Isabel, who was the center of attention as Peter Pan. Tom was a great Captain Hook, better than I thought he'd be. He wiggled his tiny moustache as he talked.

"Sure, you go ahead and eat with Hilary," Isabel said when I told her my plans. "I'll see you at the dance."

"Okay," I said, smiling. I was really glad my

grandmother was having a good time.

Hilary and I quickly ordered dinner. No matter how fast I ate, Hilary always finished first. A girl could get awfully skinny hanging out with Hilary—except for me, of course.

After dinner we hurried to the Main Lounge for the dance. Streamers hung from the ceiling. All varieties of pirates sat at tables or danced to the pirate band.

Hilary and I found a table and sat down. I studied the faces of the pirates to see if I could recognize Darren. But everyone looked so different. Many people wore full masks over their faces.

A scar-faced pirate asked Hilary to dance. I couldn't tell if it was Craig or not. I told myself I didn't care.

A bearded pirate in a full mask and a dark wig approached my table. He wore a huge navy jacket and red-and-white-striped pants.

"May I have the honor of this dance?" he said in a fake pirate voice.

"Sure," I said. It felt weird dancing slow with a stranger. As we danced I knew it must be Darren. I even faintly smelled his cologne. I giggled. He had found me even though I was wearing a moustache.

"What's so funny, my dear?" he asked in his raspy voice.

"I bet you never danced with a moustached girl before," I said.

"I never danced with such a lovely lady before," the pirate said.

"Oh, I thought I was a mermaid," I said, teasingly.

The pirate looked at me but said nothing. He doesn't want to give away who he is, I thought. How romantic and mysterious Darren was!

We danced a few more dances. My pirate danced a little slower tonight than usual. Maybe he has trouble seeing through his mask, I thought.

"Would you like a cola?" he asked when we got back to the table.

"That would be great," I said.

He chuckled. "Maybe I'd better not try to drink anything with my mask on."

"I wouldn't recommend it," I said.

"This thing is too hot anyway," he said, pulling off his mask. I gasped. It was Travis!

"Are you all right?" Travis asked.

"I thought you were . . . Yes, I'm fine," I mumbled.

"I'll be right back with a cool drink," he said.

I looked around the room a hundred times for Darren. Where was he? And why was I hunting for him when he never looked for me?

People were beginning to line up for the costume contest. I couldn't see a thing. The judges were circling the tables to make sure they didn't leave anyone out.

"Ladies and gentlemen, welcome to the pirate costume contest," said the Captain, who was dressed in a flashy satin pirate outfit.

I didn't like sitting all by myself. My eyes searched the crowd for Darren, Hilary, and the scar-faced pirate I had thought was Craig. Nobody looked familiar.

The Captain announced the winners of the costume contest, one by one. There were prizes for the funniest, the ugliest, the most famous, and the best couple. "And the best couple award goes to Peter Pan and Captain Hook," he said.

You could hear Isabel shriek all over the ship.

"Oh, my, we won!" she shouted. Everyone clapped and laughed. Tom held Isabel's hand as they went up to the stage to claim their prize.

"Are you husband and wife?" the Captain asked.

"No, I came on this cruise with my granddaughter, Niki," Isabel said loudly.

Was I glad we were in costume! Maybe no

one could see me blushing under my huge moustache.

Fortunately the band started to play again and drowned out Isabel's shrieks.

Then I saw Travis returning with two colas. "Sorry it took me so long," he apologized. "I got caught in the crowd near the band."

"That's okay," I said. "You missed my grandmother making a fool of herself."

"Oh, yeah, Peter Pan. She was funny," he said.

Just then I caught a glimpse of Candy across the dance floor. She stood out because she was wearing a hot pink pirate shirt with sequins.

I couldn't see who Candy was dancing with. Then she turned around. Darren was smiling at her and looking very handsome in a black satin shirt and black pants.

"Who are you looking at?" Travis followed my gaze.

"Candy and Darren." I tried to sound more cheerful than I felt.

"Hey, they really look neat together," Travis said. "Darren's black shirt is sharp."

"Yeah," I said. I was getting more depressed by the minute. I wished Hilary were here. She would say something extremely truthful to shock me out of feeling sorry for myself.

"Why don't we dance?" Travis asked.

I nodded and forced myself to smile. Travis wasn't the best dancer in the world. He worked so hard at it that soon his shirt was damp with perspiration.

Then I saw Hilary dancing with another pirate. Instantly I knew who it was. Nobody danced like that but Craig!

"Excuse me," I said to Travis when the song had ended. "I need some air." I ran through the dancing couples. I didn't stop running until I reached a secluded spot on the deck. A few tears trickled down my face. That shows how much I mean to them, I thought. It's our last night on the ship!

I wiped my tears away fiercely, determined not to cry. I leaned on the railing and studied the moonlight on the water.

I saw a shadow out of the corner of my eye. Before I knew what was happening, a wild pirate grabbed me and kissed me. It wasn't one of those spin-the-bottle kisses either. It was my first real, on-the-lips kiss. I was too startled to scream.

"Please forgive me, Niki. It was the costume that made me do it. But I have to admit I've wanted to do that since the first night I met you." The voice sounded awfully familiar. I recognized it as the pirate stepped out of the darkness into the moonlight.

"Craig! It's you," I gasped.

"You're not mad, are you?" he asked.

"Mad? Why would I be mad?"

"You're not?" Craig's voice cracked. "This is Craig, remember? You're not mad that *I* kissed you?"

"No, I'm glad," I said, smiling up into his eyes.

"Come on," Craig said. "Let's hurry." He grabbed my hand and pulled me away from the rail.

"Craig, where are we going?"

"There's only one thing left to do," Craig said.

"What?" I asked.

"We have to hurry so we can dance the last dance."

We rushed back to the Main Lounge. A slow song was just starting as we got there. When Craig took me in his arms, I thought my heart would burst.

"I wish this cruise could go on forever," Craig said.

"I was thinking the same thing," I told him.

Hilary was dancing with Travis. She looked from Craig to me and smiled knowingly. I smiled back and gave her a thumbs-up sign.

Unfortunately the last dance had to end.

"Wait for me. I'll be right back," Craig said and rushed over to the bandleader. I don't know what kind of persuasion Craig used, but the bandleader turned to the microphone and said, "We've had one last request. This song is for Craig and Niki."

Craig came back to me, and we danced one more heavenly dance.

Afterward, Craig walked me to my cabin.

"Good night," he said. "I had a really good time." He turned and started to walk away.

"Wait," I said. "I had a good time, too. I wish it hadn't taken me so long to realize . . . what a good time we have together."

"Maybe we can get together again," Craig said, taking my hand. "Miami is only twenty minutes away from Fort Lauderdale."

"I hope so," I said.

"You'll write to me, won't you?" Craig asked.

I laughed. "I'm good at writing letters. I've written to my friend Jenny every day."

"Good," he said. He kissed me again, then quickly turned and hurried down the hall to his cabin.

I reluctantly went inside. My wonderful pirate masquerade ball was over. I really felt like Cinderella now. My prince was leaving in the morning, and I didn't even have a glass slipper.

Ten

I woke up to the sound of Isabel's voice.

"Niki, dear, it's time to get ready for breakfast," she said softly. "Remember we have to have our bags out in the hall by nine o'clock."

"Oh, no," I groaned. "I don't feel like breakfast today. Please go without me. I'll pack while you're gone, I promise."

"Well, if you're sure." Isabel felt my forehead and slipped quietly out of the room.

I put my pillow over my head. It was strange—I hadn't wanted to come on this cruise, and now I didn't want to leave. I dreaded the idea of saying good-bye.

I sat up and looked out the porthole. I could see land and knew we would be docking in Miami soon. What was I going to say to Craig?

I put my suitcase on my bed and started throwing my clothes into it. When I saw my pirate scarf and moustache, I began to cry.

Isabel came in as I was blowing my nose.

"Niki, darling, what's wrong?" she exclaimed. "Oh, dear, I knew there was something bothering you."

I tried to explain. "I just found out how wonderful Craig is, and now I'll never see him again."

Isabel sat down beside me on the bed. "I understand how you feel," she said. "A person often doesn't realize how wonderful a friend is until they have to part."

"When I think of the time I wasted, trying to believe I liked Darren . . . and Craig was there all along," I said.

"Darren has his good points, too, Niki," Isabel said.

"I guess so," I said.

"Don't think the end of the cruise has to be the end of all your new friendships," Isabel said. "You can still remain friends with Hilary and Darren and Craig."

"I told Craig I'd write to him," I said.

"Of course, you will," Isabel said. "And you can write to the others, too."

"I guess you're right," I said.

"Tom and I are going to see each other again," Isabel confided. "He's only a phone call away."

"Then you think I'm overreacting," I said.

Isabel chuckled at me. "You might say that."

"Okay, okay, so I wish I'd picked the right boy at the beginning of the cruise," I said. "There's no harm in wanting to be perfect, is there?"

"Not at all," Isabel said, looking at me. "But there is harm in expecting yourself to be perfect."

"Okay, I get the message," I said. "So I'll finish packing my suitcase like a good, imperfect, little girl. And then I'll go say good-bye to my new friends."

"Good for you, Niki," Isabel said, giving me a very long hug. "If it's any consolation, I have a lump in my throat about saying good-bye to Tom."

"You do?"

Isabel nodded. "Thank you for coming on this cruise with me, Niki. You were a dear," she said with tears in her eyes.

"Thank you for bringing me," I said. "You know what? I'm actually hungry."

"Oh, I almost forgot. I brought you a Danish and some orange juice from the dining room." Isabel got up to get the food.

There was a knock at our cabin door. "We need to unload your bags now, ma'am," called our steward. "May we come in?"

"Oh, dear, I'm terribly sorry," Isabel said as she opened the door. "We got busy and forgot." She winked at me.

I smiled as I munched my Danish. The steward loaded our bags onto his cart and took off.

I got dressed and packed my pajamas in the small bag I would carry with me. Isabel gathered her straw baskets. After a last look around our cabin, we went up on deck.

"It will be a while before we can disembark," Isabel said. "I'm going to find Tom and say good-bye. Will you be all right?"

"I'll be fine," I said, smiling. I leaned against the railing and took a deep breath. I still dreaded saying good-bye. I scanned the crowd on the dock for my parents and Jenny. They were coming to meet us.

"Hey, Niki, where were you?" Hilary asked, coming up to me. "I looked for you at breakfast."

"I didn't feel like breakfast," I said. "Hilary, you have to give me your address. Maybe we can get together some time during the summer."

"Yeah, that would be great." Hilary fumbled in her purse for a piece of paper. "We can also write to each other."

I smiled when I thought about writing letters. I clutched the packet of letters to Jenny in my hand. I wondered whether I'd been trying to fool Jenny or myself when I wrote them.

Hilary and I exchanged addresses and promised to write.

"Take care, Niki," she said, giving me a big hug. "I'll miss you."

"I'll miss you, too," I said. "I hope we can visit each other some time."

"Of course we will," Hilary said, as if she were shocked that I could even doubt it.

"There she is. There's Niki." I heard Jenny's excited voice. I whirled around and there she was with my parents.

I giggled and hugged them all. "Jenny, Mom and Dad, this is Hilary, my new friend."

"Jenny's been my best friend since kindergarten," I explained to Hilary.

Everyone said hello, and then Isabel and Tom joined us. We had to start the introductions all over again.

I saw Darren walking along the deck with Candy. I smiled at them. Darren winked at me and spoke to Candy. They came over to say good-bye.

"So long, Niki," Darren said. "It was a lot of fun."

"Darren and Candy, I want you to meet my family," I said, feeling suddenly very free. I didn't have to try to like Darren anymore. Why had I tried to force it in the first place?

Darren said hello to my family and flashed his smile at Jenny. She was staring at him with this silly grin plastered on her face.

"I hope you wrote in your letters about *him*," Jenny whispered when Darren and Candy had gone.

"Yes, I did," I admitted. "But don't believe a word of it."

"What do you mean by that?" Jenny asked.

"Never mind," I said, smiling. "I'll explain later."

Jenny and I sat on the lounge chairs while my parents and Isabel and Tom chatted by the railing.

"Niki, there's a boy coming over here," Jenny said, poking me.

"Where?" I followed her gaze. There was Craig, holding a bouquet of carnations.

I stood up as Craig came toward us.

"Niki, these are for you," he said, thrusting the flowers into my hand.

"Oh, thank you," I said. "Craig, I want you to meet my best friend, Jenny."

"Hi, Jenny," Craig said.

"Hi, Craig," Jenny looked puzzled.

"It's really hard to say good-bye," I said, looking at Craig.

"Uh, I think your mother is calling me," Jenny said, hurrying away.

"Don't say good-bye," Craig said, taking my hand. "Think of all the good times we had on the cruise. Think about everything we have in common."

"Okay." I smiled and sniffed the pink carnations, but my eyes were glued to his. I realized how sweet he really was—how sweet he had been this whole week.

"I've been an idiot on this cruise," I said, trying to think of a way to apologize.

"Really?" Craig said. "I thought I was the idiot."

"That's one more thing we have in common, hmmm?" I smiled.

"Don't forget to write," Craig said.

"I won't forget."

"Maybe we'll discover we have more in common."

"I'm sure we will," I said as I wrote down my address for him. He handed me a paper with his address written on it.

"As soon as we get home, let's write to each other and see who gets a letter first," Craig suggested.

"Okay." I laughed. I could see the wheels

turning in his mind as he thought up the experiment.

"Niki," Isabel called. "It's time to go."

I stood up. "I have to go."

Craig jumped up. He took my hand and held it for a minute. "Let's plan to see each other again, too," he said softly. "Fort Lauderdale and Miami are close to each other, you know."

"I'd really like that," I said. I turned and walked away quickly. I didn't want to cry in front of all these people.

"How about August, Niki?" Craig called. "Let's get together in August before school starts."

I turned around and nodded, smiling at him.

Isabel searched my face when I joined her. "How did it go?" she asked.

"Okay," I said. "Since Craig lives in Miami, we're hoping to see each other again soon."

"That's marvelous, Niki," Isabel said.

"Who's that boy?" Jenny asked as we got in the line to descend the gangplank.

"You won't believe this, but he's the nerd I met the first night," I confessed. "I told you about him, remember?"

Jenny's eyes got big. "He's the nerd?"

"Uh-huh," I said. "Only you haven't heard the best part. He turned out to be a really neat guy."

"I can't believe it," Jenny said. A hundred cute guys could have surrounded Jenny at this point, and she would have ignored them. I had her complete attention, all right.

"Maybe you should read the letters," I said, handing her the packet. "Then I'll tell you what *really* happened."

About the Author

In addition to writing, BONNIE TOWNE teaches creative writing in high school and is the advisor to the school literary magazine. She lives with her husband and two teenage children in St. Petersburg, Florida.

Bonnie gets many of the ideas for her books from her students, and she admits that the personalities of her children and students often appear in her books.

When Ms. Towne is not writing books or teaching, she likes to swim, read, and walk on the beach. Other books by Bonnie Towne include *Why Doesn't She Go Home!*, *A Summer To Remember,* and *Hollywood Jr. High.*